NEVER FALL DOWN

Also by Patricia McCormick

Purple Heart
Sold
My Brother's Keeper
Cut

NEVER FALL DOWN

A NOVEL

PATRICIA McCORMICK

BALZER + BRAY
An Imprint of HarperCollins*Publishers*

This is a work of fiction based on a true story.

Balzer + Bray is an imprint of HarperCollins Publishers.

Never Fall Down
Copyright © 2012 by Patricia McCormick

Library of Congress Cataloging-in-Publication Data
McCormick, Patricia.
Never fall down : a boy soldier's story of survival / Patricia
McCormick. — 1st ed.
    p. cm.
Summary: Cambodian child soldier Arn Chorn-Pond defied the
odds and used all of his courage and wits to survive the murderous
regime of the Khmer Rouge.
ISBN 978-0-06-173093-1 (trade bdg.)
ISBN 978-0-06-173094-8 (lib. bdg.)
1. Cambodia—History—1975–1979—Juvenile fiction.
[1. Cambodia—History—1975–1979—Fiction. 2. Party of
Democratic Kampuchea—Fiction. 3. Soldiers—Fiction.
4. Genocide—Fiction.] I. Title.
PZ7.M13679Nev 2012   2011052211
[Fic]—dc23   CIP
                                                                  AC

Typography by Michelle Taormina
12 13 14 15 16   LP/RRDH   10 9 8 7 6 5 4 3 2 1
❖
First Edition

When Arn Chorn-Pond was eleven, the Khmer Rouge, a radical Communist regime, came to power in Cambodia, herding the entire population to work camps in the countryside. Families were separated, and everyone, including children, was forced to work long, grueling hours digging ditches and growing rice.

Tens of thousands of people died from starvation, overwork, and sickness. Many more were tortured, forced to swear they were traitors, then killed and buried in mass graves that have come to be called the Killing Fields.

Nearly two million people died—one quarter of the population. It is the worst genocide ever inflicted by a country on its own people.

CHAPTER ONE

BATTAMBANG, CAMBODIA
APRIL 1975

AT NIGHT IN OUR TOWN, IT'S MUSIC EVERYWHERE. RICH HOUSE. Poor house. Doesn't matter. Everyone has music. Radio. Record player. Eight-track cassette. Even the guys who pedal the rickshaw cycle, they tie a tiny radio to the handlebar and sing for the passenger. In my town, music is like air, always there.

All the men, all the ladies stroll the park to catch the newest song. Cambodian love song. French love song. American rock 'n' roll. Like the Beatle. Like Elvis. Like Chubby Checker. Ladies in sarong walk so soft like floating on the street. Men in trouser, hair slick back, smoking Lucky Strike. Old men playing card. Old lady selling mangoes, selling noodle, selling wristwatch. Kid flying kite, eating ice cream. The whole town is out at night.

My little brother and me, we stand in front of the movie palace and sing for them. We do the twist also. "Let's Twist Again, Like We Did Last Summer." Two skinny kid, no shoe, torn pants, they like it if we sing for them; they even give us a few coin.

Tonight I study the crowd, find a lady—fat one, fat like milk fruit—and slowly, slowly, very sneaky, my brother and I, we hide behind her skirt, hold on so light she doesn't know, and pretend she's our mom. Kid with parent can see the movie for free. Kid like us, we pretend.

Inside the movie palace we watch America, black and white, with airplane, shiny car, and women in skirt so short they show the knee. War movie, lotta shooting, and a little bit kissing. For the shooting, my brother and me, we clap; for the kissing, we hide our face in our shirt.

After the show, it's the best part—when we do the movie ourselves. Outside in the park, we fly the plane, shoot the gun, be the hero. Just like the real soldier fighting right now in the jungle outside of our town. We shoot probably a hundred bullet, die a hundred time. Then we hear a whistle, and the sky far away flash white. The palm tree shiver, and the ground shake. And all of a sudden the war is real.

I grab my little brother hand and run and run till we get

to a little pond near our house. We jump in, water up to our nose, and hide there. Where nothing bad can find us.

Next day, the music is back and the war is gone. Sometime the war come close, but never into our city. Most of the fighting, the radio says, it's far away, in the jungle. Government soldiers, they fight for the prince. The bad guys, I don't know what they fighting for, but I do know the prince is a great man. A great man, with important friend like the widow of the young American president. And beautiful daughter I saw in the newspaper when she and the prince go to China. So pretty, I cut the picture for my wall.

I worry about those two in China. The Chinese eat bad-smelling food. Where they gonna eat? How they gonna get home with all this fighting?

But one soldier at the market, high-ranking guy, he brag about the government fighters. He's a big, bull-neck man, this guy who says he know the prince. He says the war only gonna last one week.

He says the soldiers in the jungle, they not real soldiers. Only peasant in black pajama. Not even with real boot. Sandal made from old tire. We gonna win, he says. We gonna squish them like cockroach.

So I try not to worry about the prince and princess and worry instead about how I can make a little money.

Sometime I sell ice cream. To sell, you have to have a bell. A small bell, it sound when you walk so people hear you coming. But poor kid like me, I buy a cheap one. Old bell for buffalo. Big. Not good sound. Like old gong around my neck.

At first nobody buy. Nobody buy my ice cream because I look like poor kid. So I eat all the ice cream before it melt. Make myself almost sick. I learn a lesson then: sell fast before the ice cream melt. Sell fast. Also, go far. All over town. I walk so much I know this town like my pocket.

A lot of time kid throw stone at me. Rich kid. Kid who go to real school, with desk and a hoop for basketball. Not like temple school for poor kid like me, where you have to do chore, serve the monk, then maybe get a little teaching. Rich kid, they make a face at me, throw stones. Sometime I run. Sometime I make a face at them, too. Then run.

But soon I learn another lesson: you want to sell, you sneak out from the temple and sell when those kid in school.

My number one big sister, Chantou, she find out I'm not at the temple; she get mad. Very mad. "Arn," she say to me, "you should be doing chore for the monk, learning the chant, doing schoolwork. Selling ice cream, that's low class."

I don't tell her the monk sometime are very mean. I don't tell her they make us work all the time and that temple is not like real school. I don't tell her they get angry, they hit and say, "You stupid boy."

Also, I don't tell her we *are* low class. She still think like the old days, when our family owned the opera. My dad the star, my mom also the star. In our house, big house on the main road, before the show it was all singer and musician staying with us, getting ready. Forty people, maybe. A show every Saturday. Packed. So crowded some people have to sit on the grass. Our family a little bit rich, a little bit famous.

Then my father has a motorcycle accident. Hit his head on the road. At the hospital he yell like it's still the opera, like still onstage. Then he die and my mom, she can't run the opera anymore. She try. But no leading man, no opera. So she has to go far away, to Phnom Penh, to sing and make a little money, and we live with our aunt. Me and my brother and four sister. My aunt, she have no kid, so she love us like her own, but not enough money. That why I go stay at the temple sometime, why I also try to make money on my own.

I don't say any of this to my sister. I let her say that it's low class what I'm doing.

I want money, but also I want to have fun. Maybe it's low class. But it's okay for me.

Sometime, I steal coconuts. Sometime, the lady next door, she let me pick the flower to sell. And sometime I play a game for money. You can say it's gambling. But maybe you can say it's sport, also. Doesn't matter.

I give the head monk a little money so I can sneak out of the temple to play. You can say maybe I bribe him. Or you can say maybe I give him a little gift.

This game, it's easy for me. You draw a circle on the ground and put money there. You throw your shoe. You hit the money, you take it. I lose sometime, but most the time I win. I play not only with kid, I get so good, many time I play with the men, the cyclo driver. I tease them. I say, "You so fat, you can't see over your belly, man," and they get mad and they throw the shoe like crazy and I win.

No other little kid has money like me. This mean I can buy things for my family. Good food. Grill banana. Coconut cake. Mung bean pudding. Always I give the best thing to Munny, my little brother. Palm sugar, very sweet, wrap in palm tree leaf. But one time when I give a treat to my aunt and my sister, they cry. I don't know what's going on with them. I say, "Why you cry?"

They ask where I got this money. "A little boy like you, how you get so much money?" They keep pinching me, pinching me, and say maybe I steal it. I tell them the truth, that I win it. But they don't believe.

They go see the head monk. They take me, too, pinching my ear all down the street. "Arn got a lot of money," they say. "Where he got it from?"

The monk shake his head like this is very sad news for him. He tell them the truth, about the shoe game. And he says, "Arn try to give me some money too, but I don't take it."

I rub my ear and think: next time, no money for that guy.

In our town is a tree that make hard little seed ball. Buffalo toe tree. You shake it, the seed, they fall on the sidewalk. You cut down a reed, you stick the seed inside, you make a blow gun.

My little brother, he says tonight he's gonna shoot our sister in the butt for telling our aunt we sneak in the movie. This sister, Sophea, she's in the middle of us. Younger than me. Older than him. Our favorite for shooting at. Also she swear and says curse word when we hit her, and our aunt get mad at her instead of us.

I hug this tree, shake it hard and hear, far off, sound like thunder. I look at the cloud and wait for rain to fall like curtain, for the umbrella to pop up like mushroom. For the hot season to end and the rainy time to start.

But no rain is coming. Only truck.

All kinda truck. Mostly jeep and tank, but also Coca-Cola truck and bus and garbage truck. All full of soldiers. Young guys. Dark skin and tough, all in black. Black pajama, black cap. Only with red-and-white scarf tied around the head.

Most are kid, teenagers. Some of them only a little bit older than me. Kid with sandal made from car tire. Kid with gun. And lotta bullet across the chest. And pistol. And grenade. Some soldier are even girl. Girl with short hair, angry face.

Now people coming out of all the house. Cheering, waving white flag. Handkerchief, bedsheet maybe, scarf, everything white. They run up to the truck and try to touch the soldier.

Next to me, a guy in blue jean, hair and sideburn like Elvis, he wave at the truck. I ask him what's going on.

He says the war is over.

Up and down the street people cheer and yell and wave the flag. One guy, a cook, he wave a big spoon, also his apron. The guy who cut the hair, he shake a white towel. One old lady, no teeth, pink gum like a baby, she try to kiss one soldier.

Horn honking. Little kid, they run around in circles. Dog, even, they chase their tail. So I run around, losing myself, too. I don't know who are these guy with gun and truck, but I don't care. No more war. Maybe now the princess can come home.

All quiet now. The parade is finish, and all the people inside making food. On the radio it says, "Give the soldiers whatever you can. Show that you support them." Everyone inside now, except me. Near our house is a school, a rich-kid school, the one with the basketball game. Sometime I lean against the wall, look in the window, and try to learn like the other kid. The letter. The number. Sometime the teacher, he says scram, and I act like I don't care, like maybe I'm just passing by. But today is no school, so I kick the soccer ball in the yard.

At the corner, five black-pajama soldier stand, smoking cigarette, on a lookout. They're young, these guys, so I say, "Wanna play?"

They take the ball like they don't know what to do. They kick like they never saw this game before, and I think maybe I can make a little money off them. But also they play with a frown face, no fun, always keeping the gun on the shoulder, so I think maybe not such a good idea to gamble with these guys after all.

One soldier, the biggest one, he see a kid come by on a motorcycle, and he yell at this kid to stop. He walk to the road to talk to the kid and I go too.

He tell the kid, "Give me a turn on your moto."

You can't do that. You can't just ask someone to ride his moto. So the kid says, "No, I have to go home."

No warning, the soldier, he hit the kid in the head with the rifle. And the kid, he sag to the ground, like his leg go dead, and then fall in the curb. He twitch, and bubble come from his mouth. Then he stop moving.

I run away, very scared, very fast. I tell my aunt about this, but she doesn't believe me. She give me an orange and says to go celebrate like everyone else. But I keep that soldier in my mind.

Next day, early in the morning, no temple gong for waking up, no monk chanting. Strange sound. Voice like machine and very loud. Truck full of soldier ride down the street. Shouting in a bullhorn. "We are Khmer Rouge," they say. "We are Red Cambodia." Also, they say the prince is coming back, that all government soldier should come meet him at the airport. "All soldier of this town," they say. "Come join us." And the government soldier, they come out of the house one by one, wearing the uniform in green. Uniform, hat, boot. Even white glove, some of them. Medal also. Very fancy. Very proud. And they join the young guy in the black pajama.

One government soldier, old guy, very high ranking, living in a big house, his wife grab his sleeve so tight, he almost can't go. Another soldier's wife, young, pregnant, she wave a white handkerchief and cry a little bit. I look for the bull-neck guy, the one who says he know the prince, but no sign of him.

I follow these guys into town and run to my friend house, and throw a stone up at his window. Hong is a rich boy, and Chinese. His parents own a store, and they have a pet bird in a gold cage. He have a bike, and sometime he give me a ride on his handlebar. We go frogging in the countryside sometime, and sometime we play war. So I think maybe Hong will want to follow the soldier and maybe see the prince. Also I think maybe Hong can give me a ride on his bike.

Now Hong mother come to the window. "Get out of here," she says. "Go home." Hong stick his head out and give me a sad face. He says his family is going away. Then his mom shut the window.

They come down, carry the whole house: cooking pot, blanket, lamp, sausage on a string, record player, suitcase, rug, sewing machine, and cage with the bird inside.

"Can Arn come with us?" Hong says to his mom. "You say everyone has to leave now."

Hong's mother, she's a little bit crazy. Maybe she doesn't understand that the war now is over. But Hong's family, they also have a television, so sometime her crazy stories not so crazy.

She look at me. She look at the sausage on a string. I know this face. My aunt make this face sometime, too, when maybe not enough food for everyone.

"It's okay," I say. "I want to be here when the prince come." And in her eye I see Hong mother feel maybe a little bit relieve.

Hong hold my hand all the way to the train, then his mother push some money in my pocket. I watch the train till nothing is left but smoke in the air. Then I look to see how much money she give me. More money than from two month selling ice cream.

With no friend, no bike, I follow the soldiers anyhow. Dusty road out of town, very far, out in the country, near the frogging pond. Most the time Hong, he a little scared of frog, so I do it. I tie a little frog to the stick and wait for a bigger frog to come along and eat him. I always feel sorry for the little guy, but I tell myself that's how you catch your dinner.

But all this walking, all this dust, I get tired, so I lie down under the banana tree and take a nap. Perfect place to see the parade when the prince come to our town. Perfect place for the princess to notice me.

I think maybe I dream the war is still happening, bullet popping, ten, maybe twenty time. But when I open my eye, no noise. Only the frog in the ditch, calling his friend. And I think: let this guy go. Tonight I have money for a real supper.

Now the Khmer Rouge march back to town. But no prince. No princess. No soldier in the green uniforms either. Only Khmer Rouge. The people in town, they whisper to each other and run inside. The old wife of the high-ranking man, she fall on her knee. The pregnant wife, she hide her face in the handkerchief.

I run home to tell my aunt all of what I see, but when I get there, I see the bull-neck man; he's digging in the ground. He have on too-small peasant clothes, and he dig with his hand. And bury his uniform under our house.

The next morning, more bullhorn. Outside our house, on the main road it seem like the whole city is walking by. Thousand and thousand. Never ever I saw this many people. Everyone walking. Men, women, little children, old lady, old men. Everyone carrying rice. And blanket. And suitcase. One man, like a buffalo, with two heavy can of water on a stick across his back. Another one, whole family on his bike. Big parade. Everyone leaving town like Hong.

They go slow, the sun already hot. And I think: too bad I got no ice cream. Good day for selling.

Another bullhorn truck, driving crazy. "All people!"

the guy yell. "The Americans are coming to bomb the city!" The people on the highway, they all hectic now, running. "Prepare to leave city for three days. Go twelve miles in the country," he shouts. "In three days you will be allowed back." The soldier, he drive wild, like never he seen a truck before—this way, that way, almost into the people. "Don't be chaotic," he yell. "The Americans are coming!"

I don't understand. The American war, in Vietnam, finish a while ago. But I don't care. Today, I think, this the most exciting thing ever to happen here. Real American coming. Real airplane. I think of Hong on the train with his mother and her sausage and think: too bad he's missing all the excitement.

CHAPTER TWO

I STOP, BEFORE I RUN TO TELL MY AUNT ABOUT THE AMERICANS, and stand in front of the neighbor house. They're a rich family with a Mercedes and five girl. Girl always doing homework. Every night I see them in the window working hard, so sometime I climb up the mango tree in our yard and make a face at them.

My number one big sister, Chantou, always says to quit joking around. Rich people don't pay attention to poor people like us.

But one girl in the window, the one same age as me, the one with eyeglass, sometime she stick her tongue at me. And now I think maybe I love her a little bit. I don't know for sure about this feeling, but I think maybe she like me a little bit, too.

The father of the rich girl, he stand next to the Mercedes, and argue with a young Khmer Rouge girl.

"No car," she says. "Bicycle, okay. But no car."

The father, he has a fat wallet, and he open it. But the Khmer Rouge girl give him only a frown face and cut his tire with the knife on the end of her gun.

My aunt, she smack my bottom when I come inside. "Where you been?" she says. "We need to go. Right now." She tell me, carry this and carry that, and she point all over like crazy. My number one big sister, Chantou, she has all her college book and a sack of rice. My other big sisters—Maly and Jorami—they each carry some blanket and also food, dried fish and small banana. My aunt has a sack of charcoal and also one can of sardine. My little sister, Sophea, has a bucket of egg; and my brother, Munny, has his thumb in his mouth. I take a washtub and my picture of the princess and my peashooter, and then all of us, we all run out.

All of Cambodia is on the road. A hundred thousand people with a hundred thousand thing. Mostly rice. But all kinda crazy thing, too. One little girl, still in the white shirt and blue skirt school uniform, she carry a stuff rabbit, pink, almost big as herself. One man, he wear a suit, like in America or maybe France, and carry just one baguette, tin of sardine, bottle of wine. An old lady, she tie a rope around her stomach and pull a pony cart, her whole house in that cart. One guy has a baby pig tie to a piece of string. One old lady, she has a gold frame wedding picture and also lotta teacup.

One boy, from the school with the basketball game, he yell to me from far back in the crowd. "Arn!" he shout. "Wait up!" This guy a pest. All the time I beat him at the shoe game, and all the time he want his money back. So I pretend like maybe I can't hear him.

He grab my elbow anyhow. "My father, he went to the airport with the Khmer Rouge," he says.

This kid's father is high ranking, so probably he wanna brag now about seeing the princess or something.

"They shoot my dad," he says.

Both of us, we stop walking, even though the crowd push by us.

"How do you know?"

"My big brother, he was hiding in the bush and he saw." This kid, his eye blank, he talk in a strange voice, not like sad, like robot. "They kill him," he says. "The Khmer Rouge, they kill them all."

I understand now. Those bullet I hear in my sleep by the side of the road, they not a dream. They real.

• • •

Black smoke is up ahead. We pass through the center of town, by the movie palace, and see a big fire in the park. Where the fancy lady and man come out to stroll at night, where my brother and I do the twist, now a big pile of thing on fire: radio, television, record player, record, book—all burning.

We pass the hospital, and the sick people come out, squinty eye from not seeing the sun in so many day. All of them in blue nightgown, some of them attach to pole with liquid in a bag. One old man, his family carry him. One baby in the middle of the road, no pants, cry like crazy, but no people stop for him. The crowd, now it's like jungle, a jungle of elbow for a short kid like me. Everyone jab and push. I try to grab onto my aunt skirt, but the crowd, it sweep her away, swallow my whole family up. Then it carry me over the bridge, like my feet not even touching, and it spit me out on the side of the road.

I look back at the town, palm tree like crown on the main road, and all the flower, red and gold, like jewel, and wonder what will be left after the Americans come.

The sun is a white flame in the sky and the road all dust. Dirt in your nose, in your teeth. The boy with the dead father, he has dust in his hair, his eyebrow, so he look like an old man. I carry the washtub on my head so maybe it will make me taller, make my aunt see me better. Sometime I try to run to the front of the crowd where maybe my aunt is, but the pot so big and I'm so small, it slow me down even more. I go so slow I even lose the boy with the dead father, and now I'm with all stranger.

Next to me is a young guy with a pretty wife, long braid down her back, big pregnant belly. I walk with them and pretend that maybe I'm her son. Soon I feel the woman lean on me. She too weak even to ask, she just grab on. And so I act tough, like a strong son who can carry a washtub and also help his mother. After a while, I feel her arm lift away from me, and she slip to the wayside. The husband, he call out to the Khmer Rouge. "My wife!" he says. "She need water."

The Khmer Rouge, he only grunt. And point with his gun to go forward. The young guy open his mouth to say something more, and the Khmer Rouge hit his cheek with the gun. The guy fall over backward, and the crowd swallow him up. Him and also his pregnant wife, both are in the belly of the crowd now, and everyone just walking forward.

I learn a lesson already. Be invisible around these Khmer Rouge guys.

All the time now, people fall behind. Very slow, no noise, they drop at the side of the road. I see this and think maybe I might do this, too. I can pretend, play sick, and hide in the grass until everyone gone by. Then I can run home and maybe see the Americans and their plane.

Everybody come back to town in three day, then I'm a hero.

A ditch is next to the road. Perfect place to hide. But in the ditch, in the place I pick to hide, is an old lady lying down, like resting. Her eyes are open, but no life in them, like dead fish at the market. Everyone pass by, pretend not to see. I feel kinda scare, but I do like the other people. Inside I say to myself: so this what a dead person look like.

Hour and hour of marching and still I don't see my aunt. Along the road, lotta thing people dropped. Lotta shoe, all with no match. A suitcase split open, clothes spilling out. Sewing machine, bike, one lace sock. I drop my peashooter already, I don't remember when. Also more bodies now all the time. Some just die while they walking. Some with blood on the shirt, from the bullet or maybe the knife at the front of the Khmer Rouge gun, I think. The baguette man now is under a tree, sitting, look like taking a nap, except for blood coming out of his mouth. A little girl in a yellow dress, dirt on her dress, like people step on her. One whole family dead: a man hug his baby under him, his wife, her mouth wide-open, like still screaming.

In just one day a person can get use to seeing dead body.

Finally, at dark, the soldiers say to stop. Some people just lie down right where they stand, right on the road. Some go to the side of the road; they set up cook pot and blanket. I wander all around—sleeping mat and people everywhere, the good smell of dinner cooking here and there—until finally I see my aunt. My sister and brother all close around her, like hen and chick. Never ever in my life I'm so glad to see them. My aunt give me a little spank, like she mad, but really she trying not to cry, she so happy to see me. Then she let me sip sweet milk, Nestlé milk in the can, my head in her lap, too tired even to finish.

The next day more walking. We see more body—one, a baby wrap up, old red sarong around it, not even in the ground, just put by the side of the road. A big sack of rice on the shoulder of one fat guy, it split a little and rice spill out. He can't see, so people grab some rice from the ground. Even me. I pick some grain from the dirt, keep walking.

Now is deep country. Farther than ever I been before. Farther even than the frogging pond I go with Hong. Very beautiful here—all gold rice fields, many blue fish pond, all square, like in checker cloth, very neat, very pretty. No people in these village. Only dog eating trash.

We get to one empty field and the Khmer Rouge in charge, he says some people, maybe a thousand, can stop here, make a camp. The rest of us, he says, keep going. Another field, maybe another one thousand, can stop. This one guy, he pick who can stay and who keep walking. At the next field, he pick a man with an accordion, the kid with the baby pig. Also, he let in the boy with no father. I feel sad for this kid, no dad now, just like me, but also a little bit jealous. He can stop marching now. Also maybe he can hear this accordion sometime.

Finally, the Khmer Rouge says we can stop. He says to make a hut. "Cut down the tree, use the branch, the leaf," he says. "Eat the fruit, anything you can find. This rich guy, he own the land, he can give it to the Revolution."

I don't know what this is, this Revolution. But I think maybe this guy not too smart. The rich, they chase you if you steal their things. Poor people, they the one who share.

Three day. The Khmer Rouge say we go back to town in three day. Now it's already one week. Already New Year's passed, time for fun, for big meal, for gambling.

My little brother, Munny, he run up to a soldier and ask when we can go home. I think maybe this guy gonna get mad, but he just says the same thing as before: three day.

Munny, he wait three day, then he ask the solider again. Three day, he say. Always the same answer, even after three day already pass.

All this time and still no Americans, still no bomb.

One night, two Khmer Rouge with a little book, they come to our hut. We make it nice, a sheet on a banyan tree, big branch, soft ground, blanket all over, even one pillow.

"Give us the name in this family," they say.

My number one big sister, Chantou, she says all the name fast, so fast the guy with the pencil, he hang his mouth open, catching flies. Then he grip the pencil, like squeezing a chicken neck, like never he seen a pencil before, and make mark in his book. Mark like little kid make. Clumsy.

"Give us your background," they say. "Tell us what job you have."

My aunt says only that we sell in the market. She doesn't tell about the old days, about my family having the opera. Always she brag about this before; today she doesn't say it, I don't know why. And the Khmer Rouge, they write everything down.

"Now you grow rice," they say. "We all the same now. No more elite. Even city people have to grow rice."

They don't explain, just go to the next hut.

• • •

I follow these guy. My little sister, Sophea, she come, too. She says she gonna tell our aunt if I don't let her. Also she says she can protect me, make sure I don't get in trouble. She's skinny and a girl, but also she's brave and climb tree and know how to swear, so I say okay. We hide in the bush behind the two Khmer Rouge when they go hut to hut. Same thing each time. "Give all the name," they say. "Tell us what you do." And they write it down in the book.

Sometime they ask about other people in the camp. "The man next to you. He a teacher? A doctor? He a soldier?" they say. "Give us the names of all professional people, all high-ranking people."

Also they take people's belonging. Flashlight, pencil, toy, photograph, money, and wristwatch, always wristwatch. One Khmer Rouge guy, he take so many watch he have six or seven on one arm. One old man, I see him throw his watch in the bush before the Khmer Rouge can take it. One lady, she bury her ring in the dirt.

When the Khmer Rouge get to the hut of the bull-neck guy, this guy, he look at the ground. He give them a strange name, not his real name, and says he is farmer. One soldier, the guy who strangle the pencil, he start to write down this answer. But another guy, this guy with lotta bullet strap on his chest, he put the tip of his gun under the bull-neck man's chin. He lift his head.

"But your skin so pale, comrade," he says.

The bull-neck man, he's quiet.

The soldier with the bullet, he pretend like he now talking to the other soldier, but really he says this loud, for everyone to hear. "This is not a man who spend his days in the sun. This is a man who lie."

The two Khmer Rouge tie this guy by the hand and take him away.

The Khmer Rouge, they want the name, the background of everyone here. But the Khmer Rouge themself, they all the same. All black uniform. All grim face. All name "Comrade." Comrade Soldier. Comrade Elder. Comrade Cook.

In my mind, I give them names. The one who steal is Comrade Wristwatch. And the one who all day clean his nails I call Comrade Lazy.

But they only say "Comrade" this and "Comrade" that. Because they don't want us to know the real name.

Every day now, we all work in the field. Planting, digging ditch, hard work and in the sun. Everyone. Children, old people, everyone work together. Only time for rest is to use the latrine, maybe to get water from the stream. One time, when I take Munny to the bush to pee, I see, in the wood, big pile of dirt. A pile tall as a house. Fresh, like just dug. And not a good smell. Sweet and also like rot. Like nothing I ever smell before.

The Khmer Rouge measure rice for each family with can. Nestlé can. Half can for each family. Maybe some salt also. Our family rice almost gone. Only a little left. Like maybe twenty grain.

So my aunt, she dig a little in the earth. I think maybe for mushrooms. Maybe for herb. Maybe wild plant. Something for the soup. She come back, just a little dirt in her hand.

Only way to make it thick, she says.

The Khmer Rouge come to the hut next to us, check the little book, then tell the father to come out. They say an oxcart is stuck in the mud. "You," they say to the father. "Come help us move it."

This man is teacher, mathematic teacher at the rich-kid school. Skinny guy, thick eyeglass, no muscle, soft hand. Why the Khmer Rouge not choose a strong guy? A farmer, maybe, or a guy from the river barge?

His wife, she's crying now, but the man says to hush. Very slow, like maybe he's going somewhere important, like maybe to business meeting, he tuck in the shirt, brush the wrinkle out of his pant, comb his hair. Then he kiss each kid on the head very slow. His wife, he kiss her last. Then he leave with the soldier.

Three day go by and this guy never come back. The dirt pile in the woods, every day it get bigger. They don't explain, but I figure what they doing. They kill everyone who used to be rich or high ranking. Anyone with education. All the soldier, the teacher, the doctor, the musician. Anyone poor, no problem. World is upside down. Being rich now is no good. Being poor, this can save your life. The list in the black book, that's how they decide who live, who die.

All the time now we hear girl screaming, girl running, girl crying. At night but also sometime in the daytime. All the time, the Khmer Rouge they chase the girl, cut the hair. Sometime with scissor, sometime with knife. Chop short, to the chin, like boy. The girl, they cry and sometime they run. They run, it's no good. The Khmer Rouge maybe shoot them, maybe take them to the bushes, do whatever they want. A lot of the girl afterward, they pull on their hair, pull like maybe they can stretch it, make it long, make it beautiful again.

My number two big sister, Maly, her hair like silk. Most proud thing about her, her hair. Shiny black, like blue, like a crow has. Every night she brush her hair, every morning. Sometime even she brush her hair not thinking, just dreaming maybe about the boy she love. One morning I wake up before everyone and see her making the rice. Her neck, it's bare now, her skin there is pale, never saw the sun, her long hair gone. Last night while I was asleep, the soldier, they cut her beauty. So now when she give me a bowl of rice soup, her eyes stay on the ground.

The Khmer Rouge, today they make us go in two group. One group men, one group women. And they tell us: strip bare. My brother and me, we cover ourself, put our hand in front. One man near me, he unzip his trouser, dark blue, straight line down the front; he take them off very neat and fold them into a square. Very slow. Very scare. Then I see wetness next to his foot, small puddle of pee.

The Khmer Rouge, they take all the clothes, they check the pocket for anything they can take, then put all pant and shirt in a pile. They hand out black pajama for everyone and say get back to work. We go back to the camp and see all the women, all the girls, now also in black pajama. A thousand people all the same.

We go to work then, a thousand black ant in the rice field, and we smell the burning. All the old clothes, our old life, one big pile, is on fire now. And gone.

Many time at night the Khmer Rouge make us come to meeting. All day we work, at night we have meeting.

"Brothers, sisters," says the megaphone man. His cheeks fat like plum, his voice kindly and cheerful. Like a grandfather maybe. "Comrade, today we begin a new era of happiness. Now all of us, we live as equal, no rich, no poor."

He says all of us, we have to give away what we own. "Everything belong to Angka now," he says. Every pot and pan and bowl and spoon. "Do not be afraid," he says. "Angka will provide all that you need."

I don't know this word, *Angka*, but I know not to ask.

Then the soldier come and take everything. Pot. Pan. Blanket. Pillow. Bucket. Toy. Fishing net. Cart. Lantern. Everything. My number one big sister, Chantou, she give her college book, tear running down her face; and my number two sister, Maly, she give her hair brush. I give my picture of the princess.

Our hut is bare now. No thing in it. Only people.

That night, a big feast. Rice and fish, soup with lemongrass and morning glory. All of us, we eat together. Long table in a long hut. Plenty of food. All for sharing. The grandfather guy, he smile, like Buddha. But the soldier, they keep the gun point at us.

Next day, they wake us up to work at 4 a.m. We work until dark. Dinner is rice soup and salt.

• • •

No water buffalo at this camp, so the kid, we have to walk on the rice husk, back and forth, back and forth, till it split open and the grain come out. We pound it with our feet. Hard work. And boring. And hot. Also, tough on the feet.

One girl, short hair like all of them, she notice the guard not looking; she stick her tongue at me. I know this girl. She's from the next-door family, the family with the Mercedes. The young one. I stick my tongue back. We work longer, pounding the rice, then one time, I brush my arm on her. She pinch me next. And I think: okay, this is love.

Then, from nowhere, a guard yells, "Stop!" And we see a guy running, very fast, away from the men's group, the group that dig the canal. I know this guy. Back in the city, he flirt all the time with my number three sister, Jorami, and one time give us a free ride on his cyclo. This guy, I watch him now; he run this way and that way, and the guard shoot, but the bullet go into the air. And then he disappear into the jungle.

The rich girl, she squint like she can't see so far.

"Where your glasses?" I ask.

She make a mad face and tell me to shut up. She whisper then. "The Khmer Rouge, they kill people with glasses," she says. "Anyone with glasses must be high ranking and go to a real school." She squint at me. "The Khmer Rouge, they ask you about my family, you tell them we poor, okay?"

I look at her. Weak eye from so much book reading at night. Round tummy. Soft hand. And I think no one ever will believe that. But I say okay.

That night, everyone whisper about the runaway guy. My sister Jorami, she sit outside our tent all night, looking to the jungle, like waiting to see him. In my dream I see him. No bullet can catch him. All day he hide in the jungle; and now, at dark, he sneak out to the main road. And very slow, very quiet, he run back home.

One day the Khmer Rouge come for the father of the rich girl. They say he has special skill; they need him. We don't see him that night. The next day the whole family is gone, the soup still cooking on the fire.

My little brother, his stomach now getting bloat, full of air from no food. He cry at night, he beg me, he says, "Arn, remember the palm sugar candy you buy with your gambling money? Tell me again, what it look, how it taste." I tell him no; I tell him remembering this good food only will make us miss it more. But one time when Comrade Lazy clean his nail, I pick a little mint leaf from the field and sneak it to my pocket. That night my brother and me, we fall asleep chewing this little leaf, but in our mind is candy.

My sister Jorami, every night she sit outside and look to the jungle for the runaway man; and in the daytime she look up from the field a hundred times, always waiting in her eyes.

One old man digging a ditch, he fall down. He cry and says he's too old for this hard work. A Khmer Rouge come to him, says, "You tired of working? Okay. We take you someplace you can rest."

Never again we see that old guy. But the dirt pile, it get bigger all the time. Bigger and worse smell. Like rot. And also like some kinda gas. And flies all over. That pile, now it's like mountain.

Tonight it's another meeting. These meeting, sometime they last four hour. Always, someone talking about Angka. Sometime, you so tire, you fall asleep. But you too afraid the Khmer Rouge will see, so you sleep, your eyes open.

This night one Khmer Rouge, a high-ranking guy, he take money from his pocket and rip it into shred. I wake up for this, to see someone so crazy he tear up money.

"No need for money now," he says. "No school, no store, no mail, no religion. No thing from the American, from the imperialist. In Cambodia, now it's Year Zero."

No one can talk at these meetings. No one allowed. But one old lady, she mutter. "This guy is not the prince. The prince, he's the only one who can decide; only he can say this."

I think the Khmer Rouge gonna kill her, but the man, again, he make a Buddha face. "Angka," he says, "sees what inside your heart. The prince, he has two eyes. Angka, as many as a pineapple."

Angka. We hear this word all the time now. Angka will end corruption. Angka will double the rice crop. Angka will cut out what is infected. Angka will make Cambodia great again. The Khmer Rouge, they don't explain this word, only tell us Angka now is in charge of our country, and new rule is we have to clap when we hear this word. Not regular clapping. Everyone start at one time. Everyone stop at one time.

Three month at this place and my sister Jorami, her beautiful face now is old, her eyes not waiting anymore. The Khmer Rouge, they make people disappear all the time. My sister, she disappear little by little every day.

• • •

The Khmer Rouge, they organize everything. Then they organize it again. They make two group: base people and new people. Base people are the good one, peasants from the rural area, the Khmer Rouge say, hard and dug out of the earth like diamond. New people, city people, are bad, not pure, lazy like imperialist, like America, like lackey. Bad from soft living.

Base people get two can of rice soup, new people only one. Base people are strong. New people are weak. But in the rice field, new people do the work; base people watch.

We work this way for another month, maybe more, then the Khmer Rouge organize us again. New work unit, they say, will be men with the men, women with the women, children with the children. Each work unit will go to a different farm. Men to one, women to another. Kid like my age will go to one, kid my little sister Sophea age will go to another. Kid who are almost adult, like my three big sister, they go somewhere else. Kid who are too little to work, like my brother, they will go to school. All families now will be split; parents must give their children to Angka.

"Bring only the clothes on your back," they tell us. "Angka will provide everything you need."

Also, they say, we only will be gone for three day.

● ● ●

We all keep a stone face at the meeting. But back at our hut, all my sister, they start to cry. "No crying," my aunt says, very strict. "You cry only in your mind."

Then she hold us all in her arm. "Do whatever they say," she whisper. "Be like the grass. Bend low, bend low, then bend lower. The wind blow one way, you bow that way. It blow the other way, you do, too. That is the way to survive."

But later, when everyone else asleep, I hear my aunt, her tears, they fall like rain.

CHAPTER THREE

WE WALK THREE DAY. ONE LONG LINE OF KID, ALL IN BLACK, ONE black snake with five hundred eye. Very tire, my leg heavy like boulder, my mind think only of the next step, then one more step, just walking, no thinking, no caring. Some kid die on the way. They die walking. Some kid cry for their parent or say they tire, they hungry. They get shot or maybe stab with the bayonet. Now we don't even look. We only walk.

The rainy season is here now, and the path is like river of mud; and the nighttime is very cold with no blanket, only thin pajama, so we sleep with all of us very close to stay warm. Also it's the season when malaria can come, and all the time we get bit by bug. At night I think maybe to cry a little bit for my family, but I do like my aunt says, cry only in my mind. In the daytime very hot, like steam almost; and when we walk, I think maybe I go crazy. Because I can think of only one thing. Ice cream cone.

After all that walking, we come to a temple. A big temple in the country with red roof like wing and many building all around. Long wood building for the monk to live, for the nun, all empty now. Also a giant tamarind tree. And a pond with morning glory and whisker fish. And a mango grove. Very beautiful and quiet, very quiet, with Buddha eyes on top of the temple, watching everything.

The Khmer Rouge, they say we can all sit down, sit in this big square in front of the temple. "Angka is happy to welcome you here," says the head guy, different guy from the camp with my family; this guy has moon face, fat cheek. I don't understand how Angka can be here and also at the camp with my aunt. But this moonface guy, he can read my mind.

"Angka," he says, "is a head with four face. It follow you everywhere."

He says this camp is special. Not just a rice farm. A special place where the most high-ranking Khmer Rouge leader will come sometime. He says the leader will be watching, to see how good we work.

Then he says that we kid, we the beginning of a new society, a new country, with no memory of the past. "Do not spend time thinking about the people you left behind," he says. "Angka will take care of them."

"Angka," he says, "is your family now."

It's a long wooden building where we sleep. Row and row of kids, all the feet facing in, sleeping on straw mat. One building for the girl, one building for the boy. A kid like me, eleven years old, I'm a little bit older than the kid in my building, so the Khmer Rouge say I'm in charge. "You teach these kid to love Angka," they tell me. "And you tell us if they have poor character."

And the work now is even harder. We get up before the sun, have only a little rice soup, then work in the rice field all day, hot, hot sun burning our skin, mud coming up to our knee. No grown-up around, so we do all the work. Digging with only our hand, pulling the plow like ox, pounding the rice, everything. Very tire now from all this work, so tire, it's like we work in our sleep. At night, meeting, always meeting. And sometime even work at night.

At the meeting, always they talking about rice, about digging water canal. "With water we make rice, with rice we make new society," they say. All this talk about rice, but never enough of it for us to eat. Each night, less and less for dinner. Each day, more and more work.

Also at the meeting, they tell us how we can make ourself pure. The Khmer Rouge, they mock the city people, the new people. "Your hand too soft," they say. "Only good for holding a pen, not for hard work." And they rank us on our work. Good, medium, or weak. You weak, you have poor character. You good, maybe you get a little more food.

Many kid get sick, not enough food, too much work, maybe malaria, but the Khmer Rouge say also it's poor character, it's "disease of the consciousness." Or they say you just lazy. The kid who don't work hard, sometime they get sent to another place call the lazy village. And we don't see them again.

One time I hear a kid ask where is his sister. The Khmer Rouge laugh and say she still working in the field, "only now she fertilizer."

All the rice, finally we harvest it. We lay it out to dry, almost tasting it with our eye. So beautiful this rice, and now we will have plenty to eat.

Then the truck come and take it away.

Only a little left for us to eat. Usually thin soup, like water, so thin, in your mouth you can taste the metal from the pot. And the kid, they get more and more thin, too. Rib sticking out. And big belly, swole, like air inside.

So hungry all the time now, my stomach it eat itself, a pain like never I had before in my life. And so tire, I think sometime I sleep standing up. Other time I think maybe I will just lie down in the field; the ground, it call my name.

I see some kids die in the field. They just fall down. Maybe it's malaria. Or maybe they starve. They fall down, they never get up. Over and over I tell myself one thing: never fall down.

Today, the Khmer Rouge in charge of our crew, Comrade Frog Face I call him because of his big lip, he send me to another field with a message. I come back a different way and see buildings where you keep the horse. No horses in there now. In each stall, men. Many men, altogether maybe one hundred, all tie together like animal. Tin roof, very hot, small stall, very crowded. All waiting to go to the temple for beating, and later, for killing.

They cry, call out to me, beg for water, beg for help. Before, on the march, I learn to not see things. Now, I learn how not to hear also.

But I understand something now. Why this place is special. Not only a rice farm, this holy place; it's also prison.

• • •

Today, the Khmer Rouge does a new thing to decide who is good and who is the enemy. They classify your skin. They call a meeting and look at each kid in the face. If you have a smooth skin or a light skin, they say, "You must be middle class. You don't work in the sun." They point to their own skin, very dark, like copper, and they say, "You see, we are dark skin; we work all day under the sun. We are peasants. Revolutionaries."

I use dirt, smear it on my face so I can look dark. I do this while the Khmer Rouge look at another boy, a light-skin boy. "This one can go to the mango grove," they say. And that boy, they take him away and we don't see him again.

A few days later they have another new way to find out who is good and who is the enemy. They call another meeting and look at each kid again. People with faces a little bit Chinese—eyes like almond—they say, "Come with us." People with faces a little bit French—long nose, like a bird—they go to the mango grove also. We don't see any of those kids again.

Every day, the Khmer Rouge tell us we have to forget the past. This is Year Zero, they say; nothing has come before. All past knowledge is illegal. Also they tell us, over and over, about a new disease in the mind: thinking too much. You must be like the ox, they say, no thoughts, only love for Angka.

But inside my head I keep a door, always lock, where I hide my family. Where inside is my aunt, my sisters, my little brother, all waiting.

This night, it's raining very hard. Everyone sleeping. I don't know why, I just sit next to the window and look out. It's open window, no curtain, very dark. But I can see, at the temple, three, maybe four soldiers; one is Comrade Frog Face, the others I don't know, and one guy with his hands tied. The Khmer Rouge push him to go first. Into the rain. They take him to the place right outside the window where I am.

I hold still. Like statue. I move, they see me. They see me, they kill me.

Right away they hit him. They push him in the back, and he drops flat on the ground, blood all over him. But he gets up again; and I can see Frog Face, very mad face, hit him with screwdriver, hit him in the knee, the back, the shoulder.

The others, they push him again and his legs drop. He stumbles, falling, coming toward me. Very close to me at the window. Then he fall down. He lies close by to me now. Very close. I can smell the blood on him, like killing the chickens at the market. But I don't move. Not one hair.

Now they drag this guy under the tamarind tree. They make him like he's sitting down, put a helmet on his head, an American helmet, and they light a cigarette and put it in his mouth. They laugh, then they gone.

This guy, he look right at me. Eyes open. But dead. Already dead.

I think maybe I gonna feel sad or maybe scare. But no feeling in me. No crying. I don't care about anything. Death is just my daily life now.

We kids, so hungry now, we hunt for food for ourself. Insect, frog, maybe mushroom or plant. So many kids crawling for food all over, maybe three hundred kids still living, it's hard to find this food. And some kids, lotta kids, eat poison plant, maybe spider, and die. Me, I eat the tamarind fruit. Very sour and very good. But also give you diarrhea. Already I have diarrhea, but I can't help it; I still eat the tamarind. You eat some, your mouth wrinkle up inside, and you want some more. You eat more, your stomach pain you so much, you can't stand straight.

All the kid have diarrhea now. With this diarrhea, you feel like you have to shit a hundred times each night. You so tired, you work all day, you almost think, maybe I can just shit right here in my bed. Some kid do. Then Khmer Rouge get very angry, beat them. So you don't care how tired, you get up. You go to the latrine, and it's crawling with maggot; just one board, very slippery, over a ditch,

45

also crawling with maggot. Some kid so weak, they fall in. I think they die too.

Seems like a hundred times each night, you shit. But nothing comes. Only like water. And you go back to bed, but all around you, kid crying, kid moaning. One little boy next to me, always he cry for his mother. No way you can sleep with this sound. You do sleep, you have a nightmare: you see killing, dying, same as in the day. And soon it's time to get up and go to work.

You not allowed to go around by yourself at night. Khmer Rouge see you, they think you trying to escape and they shoot you. But night is when I get most hungry, so I sneak out and try maybe to catch frog or cricket. No time to cook, only to eat fast. Sometimes I can feel the cricket legs running, running in my throat, trying to live.

One night, I go down the path to the mango grove. I don't know why I go, hungry, maybe, but curious, too. I just go. I know what I think I'm gonna find, and I find it. Big dirt pile and bad smell, very bad. Ghost, also, I think, and I run back to bed.

Sometime when we work in the field, I grab my stomach and tell Frog Face I have to run behind a bush to shit. It's not true, just a trick for taking a little break in the shade.

I make a sick face, drop my work, and run fast, fast, fast, like maybe I will shit in my pants if I don't go to the bush right away. Anyone can do this trick, I think, but no other kid think of it or maybe they too afraid. I hide in the bush as long as I can, watch them still working very hard, hot sun, no rest, and I don't feel anything. Not sorry. Not shame. Maybe even a little proud.

Then one day a boy in my group—this boy, he want the Khmer Rouge to like him and so he work very hard, always first to start, last to quit, big smile all the time— he tells Frog Face I have bad character. He says I'm a faker. He says he counts how many times I go to the bush, more than everyone else, he says.

Because of my bad character, the Khmer Rouge send me for education. This education, it's not in school. It's sleeping three nights in the manure pile. Three nights, very bad smell and always feeling bugs crawling in my clothes. By myself and very scared. Scared of ghost, scared also if I don't do this thing—lie in the manure— the Khmer Rouge will come and shoot me.

Three nights not sleeping is lot of time for thinking. I think two things: when I come back, I will find the hard-working boy. I will smile very big at him, in front of Frog Face, and tell him thank you for helping me see my poor character. Also I will watch this guy, watch him every minute, catch when he does a bad thing. Then I will say

to him, "I know what you do, but I'm not telling on you."
And then I will say, "You will not ever be telling on me
again."

New guy in charge our group today. No more Frog Face.
No explanation about where he goes. Looks like the
Khmer Rouge even make other Khmer Rouge disappear.

Another meeting. This time, the high-ranking Khmer
Rouge guy says, "Who can play music?"

No one, not one kid, make a move.

He says there will be a new music troupe, a band to
play songs. And dancer, too.

We all still, like rocks.

I think maybe this is test, new way to find out who is
elite, who has education and music lesson. Or who likes
the American imperialist and their lackey singer.

They say the band will play for the glory of Angka.
Song and dance. To cheer the worker and teach new ideas.

Maybe, I think, maybe you play these song, maybe
they feed you a little more. This is like gamble. Like
the shoe game back home. You throw the shoe, you eat
better.

I raise my hand. Just give me one bowl of rice, I think,
then you can kill me.

• • •

They choose six boys. Stick boys, so skinny. And they take us to a wood building where this old guy, white hair, white beard, sits on the floor, instrument all around him.

The Khmer Rouge say we have to learn these things in five day only. We also have to work in the field, they say, like the other kid, so the music lesson can be only at night.

The old musician, he gives me the khim. Wooden instrument with many string, string you hit with a bamboo stick. You sit on the floor and play, and it give a beautiful sound, like heaven. I hit the right string sometime, the wrong string sometime, but always I hit it too hard.

"Touch it light," says the old man. "Like hummingbird wing." Also he says, "You have talent. Work harder."

All these Khmer Rouge song are fast song, fast and happy-sounding, and all about the Revolution. About sacrifice. About hard work. About rice. Always rice.

Next day, I work in the field all day like the others, then go to the old man. Three day more only. Three day to learn this thing.

I almost cry one time, it's so hard. But the old man, he whisper in my ear. "Learn fast," he says. "You don't learn, they gonna kill you."

I work very hard now, even harder. This khim, it has

so many strings they swim in my eyes and I play very fast, hit one string, then another, so fast I can't see my own hands going. So fast, so many times, I know all the song in my heart.

The other boys, they can't do it. Next day the other boys, they don't come to class.

The old man, he spend two more days teaching me. Then one day he say, "Now that you learn the songs, they gonna kill me."

I tell him, no, the Khmer Rouge need him to lead the band.

He just smile, very sad, and tell me all the other music teacher already dead. He's maybe the last one. The Khmer Rouge don't want anyone who know the old song. All those old song gonna die out, he says.

This guy, he save my life, and now he will die. And nothing I can do to stop it.

The next day, he doesn't come. The Khmer Rouge appear then and say to me, "Come to the mango grove to see the old man. See what we do to him."

I say I don't want to see.

I don't know how I can say this. You don't say no to the Khmer Rouge.

But it's gamble. If Khmer Rouge kill me now, they don't have anyone to play their song. I think for a minute what my aunt say about how to survive—bend like grass—but this time I don't bend. I stand a little tall.

They go away, and I just play the song alone. I think of the old man, and I play for him in my mind, scared, but also in that moment, proud.

Other boys come now to the building where I learn music. One more khim player, one guy who can play fiddle call tro sau toch, one guy with a drum, and others with instrument like I used to see when my family has the opera. A new music teacher come, too, not so old, but this guy is like walking dead man. Very sad, like broken heart, nothing living in his eyes.

We gonna be a band now, the Khmer Rouge tell us. No more working in the field; now we play music all the time. Soon a big meeting is going to happen at this camp, so we have to be ready. Ready to play the song perfect. For high-ranking Khmer Rouge. We have one month to learn.

We practice music every day now, but never does it sound like a song. More like animals all calling out, all different times, and very slow, not like the old music teacher taught. The kid in the band, they all too tired, too hungry to give attention to the song; and this new music teacher, he look asleep all the time, like nothing can make him care. Not even this big meeting coming. And I think: all this work—learning the khim, learning the song—and we all will die anyway.

One night the girl next to me at dinner, she dies. She dies just sitting there. No sound. Just no breathing anymore. All of us, we eat so fast, no one even see this girl. Very quick, I take her bowl of rice and keep eating.

"You," says one Khmer Rouge to me. "You come with me."

It's nighttime, the other kids working in the fields, big torches burning so they can see. The harvest coming soon, so everyone has to work extra. Except the band. Our job is only to practice more. But this guy says, "Different job for you tonight."

He take me on one path, then another, then the path to the mango grove. Dusty path, so many feet walk down here on the way to die.

All these days I don't think of my aunt or my brother and sisters. Too dangerous to miss them and maybe cry or go crazy or just give up. But now I speak to them in my mind. I say good-bye; I say I will see them again someday. Because I know what this moment means.

Already I can see the dirt pile. Tall grass, very green. Bones sticking out: leg, arm, skull, also pieces of cloth. Also I see a ditch. And a line of people—maybe fifteen, maybe twenty—all hands tie behind, kneeling. And high-ranking Khmer Rouge standing behind them.

Then this guy, he take the ax, small ax like for chopping, and he hit one kneeling guy on the back of the head. The guy fall down, like just a pile of rag hitting the ground, very fast. Then the Khmer Rouge, he go down the line, hit each one. Terrible sound, like cracking a coconut, only it's a human head.

"You," he says to me. "You put them in the ditch."

I don't want to do this, but I do it. My body does what this guy says. I push the people, very heavy, lot of blood. I push them into the grave. I do it. One guy, he's not even dead. They say to push him in anyway.

Then the guy with the ax, he look at me. Deep in the eye. To see what I feel.

I make my eye blank. You show you care, you die. You show fear, you die. You show nothing, maybe you live.

CHAPTER FOUR

THE BAND, IT'S STILL NO GOOD. WE FORGET THE WORD ALL THE time, we play too slow, then too fast, then we play all different times. No beat. No beat at all, because the drum guy, he so scare, his hand shake all the time. And the new music teacher, he can't hear it. He always look like crying in his mind. No tears on his face, but all the time sad, no life in him, only sadness.

So I lead the kid. I try to show the drum guy how to keep the beat. Also I help the other khim player, kid name Kha—skinny kid with elephant ears that stick out on the side—I show him how to hit the string like the old music teacher teach me. "Touch it light," I say, "like hummingbird wing."

I think of the old music teacher. How he gave me, in one week, his whole life. I don't know music, only what he taught me, but maybe I can try to teach these kid a little bit and we all can live.

No rice for a few days now, and many kid are dying. Already they look like skeleton, lying on the straw mat with flies crawling in the eyes, the mouth, like already they're dead.

Tonight, Khmer Rouge say, we get special dinner. Black stew, sour smell. We know what this is. This food for pig—banana peel, rice husk, and all rotten thing. But we eat it anyway.

One song the band is learning, it's about the bright red blood that is spill to create a new land. I tell the kid to sing this song smiling, showing all the teeth, so it shows we love Angka. I sing loud, extra loud to show the way. Kha, the kid with elephant ears, he like my shadow; he copy everything I do. But the other kid, they don't learn so good.

Beside, I can't teach the music, the very hard instrument like fiddle, like xylophone; and so the song, they still not right. Big meeting in two week and still we not ready.

Kid dying from no food, from malaria, they die slow, they moan, they cry, they ask for death to come. We don't learn the song, we go to the mango grove. Death there is quick. Either way, it's death.

One night I see Khmer Rouge guy, the one from the mango grove, and he ask me how the band is going. I tell him it's very good.

He touch the small ax on his belt and his eyes go small, like lizard. "How's the new music teacher?" he says.

I don't blink one eyelash. "Very good," I say. "Excellent."

He let go of the ax. "You will tell me about this guy; you will tell me if he has bad character."

I say I will.

That night I go to the building where the new music teacher sleep. Very dangerous thing to do. To be out at night. If I get caught now, I can say, "Sorry, I can't find the latrine." But if this new music teacher can't teach us, if we play bad in front of Khmer Rouge meeting, no chance to be sorry. I know this now from the mango grove.

This guy not really asleep, just looking far away into air. I shake him, say, "Wake up. They gonna kill you if you don't teach us to play good."

He says he doesn't care. He says already he's dead in his heart. His children, all dead; his wife, he doesn't know where she is. Once before he already prepared to die, after his baby boy starve to death. He lit incense, pray to Buddha, and wait to die himself. Then the Khmer Rouge tell him to come be a music teacher. No choice. He goes. But he hate this music, this music about blood and about hard work, about the glory of Angka. He refuse to learn it.

"So they can kill me," he says. "It's okay."

I hit this guy with my fist. "Okay if you die!" I say. "But what about us? You don't teach us to play, we die too. Us kid. Like your kid die, we will die also."

Now he wake up. First time any light in his eye.

The next day this guy, he different. He still hate these Khmer Rouge song, I can tell. He grit his teeth and make a frown face. But now he really teach. He show one kid how to hit the xylophone, show the fiddle player how to make a good sound, not screeching like a cat. And now the band, it start to get better.

I think a minute about the first music teacher. I never even ask him his name. Because too short of time. That guy, he save my life, but nothing I could do when they kill him. This new guy, I ask what's his name.

He look at me like I'm crazy. No one says the name anymore. We all just comrade, we all just workers, all the same, no name, no personality.

"Mek," he says. "My name was Mek."

This guy, Mek, he decide to live because of what I say. Now, I know, it my job to keep him living.

Now the band, it get better every day. And every night I give a little of my soup away. One night to the drum player, another night to Kha. These kid think maybe I'm crazy. "Why you give us your food?" Kha says.

You can say maybe it's a gift. Or maybe you can say it's also payment for my life. These kids eat better, maybe they learn the song better. They learn the song, the Khmer Rouge let us live. They can live, I can live, we all can live. They don't learn the song, none of us can live.

The camp leader, big moonface guy, he come to the building where we play the music. Glorious news, he says. Big meeting is in one day. More good news: tonight, the band, we can have one extra bowl of rice so we can be strong and give glory to Angka.

This rice is real rice. Not rice soup, rice water. Rice to chew. White and sweet. We eat it slow, like maybe not believing it's real. But Kha, he eat it all very quick, like never again he's gonna see this kinda rice. Me, I eat some now, put some in my pocket. Because this good rice, I know it can be like money. You save it, maybe you can use it to get something later you need.

All night we practice, only a flashlight from Mek to see what we doing. We make many mistake and stop many time because a couple kids sick in the stomach from this good rice. Kha, he's the worst; many times we have to stop so he can shit. We see it, his shit, we see rice in it, not even chewed. And Kha, he cries, so much pain, and all his rice is wasted.

You think maybe you feel sad when you see this, kid in pain and also so scare for the big meeting. But instead you feel like angry, like he can get us all kill for this stupid thing he does. But after all the kids, they fall asleep playing, too tired, too sick to practice anymore, I wake Kha up, give him some of the rice I save. Little bit at a time, very slow, I tell him to chew it good.

"You play good at the meeting," I tell him, "later I give you more."

Tonight is the big meeting. The Khmer Rouge with the little ax, he comes to the place where we practice and tells us to come now. All the big leader here, and they want to hear us play. Now. Right now. Kha, he wet his pants. We all can see it. Mek, he goes pale. The Khmer Rouge, he put his hand on his ax.

I tell him it's okay, we know the songs.

Right away he take us to a wooden stage in the middle of the grass. Kha, this boy who is my shadow, walk so close he like in my pocket. Mek, he hang his head like walking to his death. All around us dark. But we can see people already sitting on the ground, thousand people, waiting for the show, all Khmer Rouge, with gun, with ax, with suspicious face.

Mek, he whisper in my ear. "You lead," he says. "I can't remember."

I close my eye and hold the bamboo stick in the air. "Touch it light," I hear the old man say. "Like humming-bird wing." I let the stick drop, and one note, one tiny ping, float into the air.

I wait a thousand year in that next second and then Kha join in, then one second later, the other kid. We play, we finish the song, we don't wait, we start another one, then another and another. We play all the song, no stopping, just playing. Only playing, not even hearing. We play, we sing, we smile—big big big, all teeth, all gums— we sing how we love Angka, how the blood was spill to set us free, how happy we are now to live in this land of plenty.

And then all the song are finished and we have no more. Only quiet. A gecko, high in the tree, he screech. Silence again.

I can see in the dark many Khmer Rouge, all waiting, all watching to see what the most high-ranking guy will do. I study this guy. I stare at his hand. I don't hear any clapping, only see hand moving. His hand, then all the hand. And we live one more day.

I sneak into the building where Mek sleep that night. Not so scare to be out at night now. I think the Khmer Rouge won't shoot me, now they like our music.

I wake Mek up, tell him he save us kids. All of us. He save us from dying.

But he says I save the kid, and him, too.

I think this might be a little bit true, but also I know in my heart I'm saving myself. "It's only surviving," I say.

Mek says he survive by dreaming. Sometimes even when he's awake. Same dream every time. He dream of a place where the children don't have to work in the field, where they sleep on the grass, and in the sky a spirit fly by and drop sugar on them.

When he wake up, he think of his own children and wonder if maybe it's better to die. "To live with nothing in your stomach and a gun in your face," he says, "is that living or is that dying a little bit every day?"

New rules after the high-ranking Khmer Rouge leave. Now no one can hunt for food. Eating by yourself is a sign of bad character, that you love yourself more than you love Angka.

Another rule: no boy can fall in love with a girl. No

girl can fall in love with a boy. Only thing you can love is Angka.

Also the band, we play song sometimes at the nighttime meeting now. So the other kid can learn the word. So they can sing how much they love Angka.

Many time when I play I keep my eye close. You look out the window, you can see the other kid working in the field, so tire, so hungry, almost dead. You see this, you think maybe you will feel sad. But you don't feel anything. Only relief that you can be inside playing music, not working in the field.

One time I open my eye and see in the field the Khmer Rouge hitting one boy, very skinny, very sick, trying to dig with his hands. The Khmer Rouge hit him and say, "Why you so lazy?" This is the hardworking boy, the boy who one time said I had bad character, the guy who got me sent to manure pile. This boy, he still work the hardest, always wanting the Khmer Rouge to like him. Now he fall down in the mud.

These Khmer Rouge, they are monster. I watch this boy fall and for one minute I feel like happy, relief that this boy is now the one in trouble. Then one minute more and I think: maybe now I am monster also.

A guy from my old town, he come to our camp sometime. He Khmer Rouge now, and he travel around to all the camp bringing the message to the leader. He says he can also give you news or maybe letter from your family. "You give me your dinner," he says, "maybe I give you a letter." To the girls he says, "You come alone with me to the woods, I tell you about your family."

I give him the last of my good rice, and he give me a letter from my number one big sister, Chantou. She says, "I'm at a mountain camp where I been sent with Maly and working hard. We both are fine here but no one knows where is our other sister. I write this letter in secret so no one knows I have education. They try to make me marry Khmer Rouge, but I say no. I will not marry, not till I see you again. Take care of yourself, little brother, and be brave until I can see you again."

Very dangerous to have this letter. Danger, too, just to think about her. You can't trust yourself to have a memory. Because these Khmer Rouge, they can see inside your head.

All the time we get extra job after practice; cook, clean—whatever they say, we do. Today I'm very lucky to be cook, because maybe I can sneak myself a little taste.

The soup we make, it's like water though. Only a little rice, maybe two, three can, for all these kids. All the rest is water. You eat it, you pee right away. No shit. Only water comes out even when you shit.

We feed all these kid in line, all these hungry kid,

these kid working so hard. But I save one small bowl for myself. One extra taste for me. Just this one time. In a hiding place under the stove. Then when all the kid done eating, I look to see that no Khmer Rouge is watching. Even in the grass behind the kitchen, sometime they put a little kid to spy. He catch you, you beg him not to tell; you say, "You can have my food." He eat your food. Then he tell on you anyway.

No kid is watching. No Khmer Rouge either. Just a tall figure in black. A big guy, but very skinny. Cheek like hollow, eye pop out. Like almost dead. In the grass, looking for food. This guy is a runaway, maybe from the prison. I don't know why I do it, but I put the bowl of rice in front of him. "Please eat quickly," I say. I don't know why I'm giving this to him. I'm hungry myself. Very hungry. I just do it. I go away then. If the Khmer Rouge catch this guy eating, I want to be nowhere around. I come back after a while. The bowl is empty. The guy is gone.

All the time I can smell the good food cooking for the Khmer Rouge. Chicken, fish, cardamom, and lemongrass. Sometime even palm sugar I can smell. The Khmer Rouge, their faces get fat and shiny from all this good food. The kid, their face pale, skin thin, like paper.

• • •

New kid come to our camp this week and one girl, she refuse to cut her hair. So the Khmer Rouge, they take her to the temple step, to a large drum on a wooden stand. They put her inside this drum and beat it. Inside, you can hear her scream. Then they make a small fire under the drum, and you can hear her cry more.

Finally, they let her out; and she has blood coming from her nose, from her mouth, from her ear, and her hair is all crazy like ghost.

"So," they say. "You still want to be beautiful?"

Everything on a schedule here. Waking up, peeing, working, eating. New schedule now for work in the rice field. Wake at 1 a.m., work till 7 a.m. Rest one-half hour. Work again, 7:30 till 11:30 a.m. Soup, then work again 1 p.m. to 5. Then at night, meeting. Always meeting.

Do this again the next day.

Every day the Khmer Rouge take six, maybe ten people to the temple. One time in the morning, one time after noon, one time in the evening, they take people from the stable. Men, mostly, but also women. Hand tie behind, head hanging. The Khmer Rouge say, "Confess, tell us what you did before. You were doctor. You were teacher. You were government soldier. You were pro-American. You spy for Vietnam." And they hit, sometime with a big stick, hit hard. Sometimes they whip with wire and the people cry, they scream. "Yes, yes," they say, "we confess." Maybe not even true what they confess, they just say it so maybe the hitting will stop.

Also three time a day we hear the little ax hitting people in the head. One time in the morning, one in the afternoon, one at night. Sometime screaming, too, and then we hear the crack, like splitting coconut. After that, quiet. Small sound, cracking the skull, but you can hear it everywhere. You hear this three time every day. Even the killing on a schedule.

Sometime the kid in the field, they stop working when they hear these sound. They turn their head when they hear the scream. Or maybe they shake a little when they hear the ax. One boy, he jump like a rabbit every time. This sound comes many times each day, but every time the boy, he jump. And always the Khmer Rouge soldier, kid like us, they watching, always with the gun pointing.

One soldier, he yells at the boy who jump like a rabbit. "Stop that," he says. "Get back to work." But the boy can't help it. His shoulder, they squeeze tight to his ear each time he hear the ax. So the soldier, he just shoot the boy. The other kid, they try not to notice. "You look, I shoot you, too," the soldier says.

Another Khmer Rouge comes to see what happened.

He doesn't say, "Why you shoot that kid?" He says, "Why you waste a bullet?"

We play our music all the time now. Same schedule as the kids in the field. No audience. Only a microphone. And we hear the music two times—one time when we play it. Another time, one more beat later, from loudspeakers, up high on a wooden post. All over the camp, our music play now.

A soldier, Comrade Rat I call him because of his big teeth, he sit behind Mek, one hand on his gun. "Play fast," he says. "No stopping." So we play and play and play, same songs, faster, faster, all the time faster. Until one time, Mek, he forget what song is next.

He goes pale. Comrade Rat, he jumps up, yells at Mek. "Play," he says. "Hurry up. Right now."

But Mek, he only stares in the air.

Then we hear it. A skull breaking.

I hit the string of the khim. One note and the others come in. Comrade Rat sits down. And Mek, he wipes sweat off his head.

I understand now: the music, the Khmer Rouge make us play so no one can hear the killing.

CHAPTER FIVE

SOMETIME WHEN THE KHMER ROUGE BRING THE PRISONER, new prisoner, I see people from my hometown. Every time, I hope I don't know these people, because I don't want the Khmer Rouge to see. They see me looking at a prisoner, they think maybe I'm bad, too.

One day I see this guy from my hometown, the taxi driver, the one with the big belly, the one I gamble and beat. Same guy, but skinny now, no belly, skin sagging off his bone. I see him kneeling in the square, his hands tie behind, and I think: this guy can get me kill only by looking at me. So I rub dirt on my face, make it very dark, and look only at my feet as I walk toward him.

Just when I get close, I look up. I don't know why. I can't stop my eyes. And I see this guy look right at me. But his eyes blank, not seeing anything, not me, not this kid who one time tease him and take his money. And I think: now two times I beat this guy. Why he dies and I live?

Today the camp leader, moonface guy, he says our band is going on a trip. We know what this mean. It means the mango grove. Never do the Khmer Rouge say, "We're gonna kill you." Always they say something else, like "Help us with the oxcart" or "You going to a new place," maybe so people don't scream and cry and beg.

You scream or cry or beg, they kill you right away. You say nothing and just go with them, they kill you anyway.

I try to think of my family—my aunt, my sister, my little brother—to hold them in my heart before I die. I try to open the lock door in my mind where I hide them. But I can't do it. I can't see them anymore, I can't make the faces come back.

All this time I work so hard to hide them; now I can't find them. All this Khmer Rouge talk of forgetting, always I think I can disobey, always I keep my family alive in my mind. But now the Khmer Rouge, they win. They kill the family in my mind.

● ● ●

They take us to a truck, and we drive a long way, out in the country; and we wonder why not the mango grove, why take us far away to kill us?

Kha, my shadow, he hold my one hand; the drummer, he hold the other one. Mek says to one Khmer Rouge, "Where you taking these kid?"

The soldier, he says, "We gonna play the song in a new place."

Mek hang his head. We know this new place. It's like the lazy village for kid who don't work hard. Or the resting village for old people too tired for working. People go to a new place, they don't come back.

We drive to an empty field; and the leader, he says to get out. All of us, already like ghost, we do what he says; we walk where he point, to a dirt hill, small, with grass, tall and green, growing on it. We know this dirt pile. Always the dirt pile with dead bodies inside; the grass there grows very tall, very green.

Ten step we walk. Eight. Six. The pile now is only four step away; and my neck, it shiver, like a chill, ready for the ax. Only two step more.

The moonface guy, he yells stop, very loud, very angry. Right away I kneel down. I know what happens if you don't kneel; the Khmer Rouge make you die extra slow, maybe cut the liver out, and you die watching it wiggle on the knife.

"Idiots!" he yells. "Go back to the truck."

We get up slow, like maybe this is a trick.

"Hurry," he yells, very mad now. "Go back and get your instrument."

Again we do what he says. The Khmer Rouge, sometime they say one thing, then they say the opposite; you just do it.

"Idiots!" he says again. "How you can play the song with no instrument? How you can entertain the worker?"

He points now to long line of men coming from behind the hill, all in black pajama, all cover in mud from digging the ditch. These workers, all very quiet, they sit down, one row, two row, many row.

So what the guy on the truck says is true: we really are gonna play the song in a new place.

Another trick by the Khmer Rouge: to always keep us afraid and also confuse, sometime they tell the truth.

Now many workers come, sit down, legs crossed, on the grass. The head guy, he tell us to play a new song, the one about the workers in the field.

"Every day is like a holiday time," we sing. "Good songs and shouts of joy ring out on every side as the peasants work the field. The earth can be hard as stone, and the sun may burn like flame; but nothing can be as strong as our love of Angka!"

"Hurrah for the new Kampuchea," we sing, "a splendid, democratic land of plenty."

We sing this, and the men, all like skull face—big cheek, eyes hollow, teeth sticking out—they clap. No smile on the face, only hand clapping, all starting together, all stopping together.

For many days we travel like this, to lotta different camp where people work. Sometime the workers all men, sometime all women, sometime kid and women together. The head guy from camp, he goes with us and ties us up, our feet tie to each other, so at night when we finish, even when we sleep, we can't go anywhere, not even the latrine. And we can smell the good food he eat, he and the head guy at each camp; they eat meat all the time—meat, fish—and maybe sometimes rice wine. We can smell this good food, even in our dream.

One boy, he sing not smiling, just moving the mouth. Also, he make mistake a lotta time on his instrument. This boy small, younger than me, very good musician. But now he has a fever half the time. Fever, then half the time shaking with cold. Malaria, I think. I give this boy my shirt for sleeping, but still his teeth knock together at night.

One day the head guy sees this kid playing the song

like he's asleep. He says, "Come with me. I have medicine for you." And that boy, we never see him again.

When we get back to the temple, the kitchen girl, she tell me to wait at the end of the line, then she give me extra food. She says I'm a little bit famous now, from playing the khim. She says the Khmer Rouge like our music. She says more high-ranking guys are coming here to hear us. She says all this good thing, but I stay modest. You act too proud, it means you love yourself more than Angka.

But I stay, sit on a rice sack, and talk with her. You could say maybe I flirt a little bit. Or you could say I also get her mind on me and not on her job while very slow, very sneaky, I pick a hole in the rice sack.

She says the top guy, the leader of the camp, he likes her, like girlfriend, like wife; that's how she know they like our music. He very jealous, she says. "He see us together, we both dead."

Then I say, "Look behind you. Is that guy watching you?" She look away, and quick I put one handful of rice in my pocket.

I keep this rice in my pocket a long time. I pass many Khmer Rouge, guy who can kill me if they find it. But I know one thing: don't act scared. You look scared, you must be hiding something. You hiding something, you better look blank.

At the meeting tonight, I sit next to little kid who sleep near me, the kid who cry all the time at night, cry for his mother. I hold very still. Like statue. My hand next to his. My eyes straight ahead. Slowly, slowly, grain by grain, I hand it off to him.

One day, all of a sudden, a new guy is in charge of this camp. A guy in white shorts, no shirt. First person I see in more than one year not wearing black pajamas. No explanation about the other leader, about where he goes. Only at the meeting at night, this new guy in white, he says the enemy of Angka are everywhere. He says we already kill all the enemy from outside; now we have to kill the ones inside. Like cancer, he says, we cut them out.

Now, with this new leader, new kind of meeting. Every week you talk about your character, about how hard you work last week. Also you have to confess anything bad you did last week. Waking up too late. Being a lazy worker. Hunting for food. After you say your confession, you have to say, "Now I am very glad to listen to all my comrade also discuss my bad character."

Anyone who acts bad goes for "education." Education, now it's not just sleeping in the manure pile. Those kid now, they don't come back.

Now no one can trust. Some guys, they lie; they make up bad act about other people to punish them or maybe just to look good for the Khmer Rouge. Even your friend, if he sees you not working too hard, he has to say it or he can be punish. All suspicion everywhere, all the time now.

Next day, some new kid come to our camp. Dancer. Dancer who march and smile and sing about Angka. I learn these dance step, too, just volunteer myself so I can be in the dance show and also the band. So maybe I can get a little more famous. Because if I'm famous, everyone know me, maybe the Khmer Rouge won't kill me.

We practice for many days, hot days, doing one big dance. We march and smile and sing about the harvest, how joyous we are, how we love Angka. End of the song comes and we freeze like statue, like picture of harvest. Each time, I kneel, like picking rice, and I get right up front so high-ranking Khmer Rouge will see me.

But every time with this song, the big guy, the one holding the flag, he also come to the front. And every time I kneel, he put the flag in front of my face. Every time.

"Hey, man," I say one time. "Move that flag out of my face."

He's a tall guy with big slow feet like elephant and big sad face also like elephant. He says sorry. He says he gonna remember next time. But when the song ends, same thing. The flag over my face.

That night, again, the kitchen girl give me extra food. She says I'm a star in the show. I stay and maybe flirt a little bit. Also, I steal some rice for the big guy who always forget and put the flag in my face. Rice and also a corncob. So maybe his stomach can remember.

That night, I dream of fish stew. My favorite thing to eat. Smell like heaven and taste like nothing else. When I wake up, it's like I can really smell it. So I sneak out to hunt for it. I can't help it; I go.

In the square I see this new guy, white shorts, no shirt, and six soldier. Also ten guys down on the knees, hands tied, all naked, in a row. The guy in the white shorts, he has a gun with a knife attach, a bayonet. He point the bayonet at the chest of one guy in the row. Then very quick, he slice the skin and pull out the liver. So quick, so neat, the liver, it stick on the end of the knife. The kneeling guy, he's still living; his liver not inside him anymore—in front of his face. Crying, only saying "No, no, no," then he fall down.

The guy in the white shorts, he do this to each man

in the row. Like butcher, he cut each one and pull out the liver, the spleen, the heart.

Blood everywhere. The white pant, the bare chest, all blood.

I see all this, smell the blood, like raw meat. And my eyes see it. But I don't feel anything. If you feel, you go crazy.

A new guy bring the letters now. The old guy, he's gone because one time he take the wrong girl to the woods. The girl of a high-ranking Khmer Rouge. We don't see him ever again. The new guy, also from my town, is kind, like a grandfather. This guy doesn't eat the kid food. He just give the news.

He tell me my number one big sister, Chantou, died. By sickness. In a hospital. But I think maybe he doesn't want to tell me the truth. I think he doesn't want to hurt me. I know these Khmer Rouge. Most of the girl, they do whatever they want with: they rape, they kill. I don't trust that she died in the hospital. But I try to believe it.

I walk away from this guy, my leg like water. I trip a little, and maybe for one minute I think I will fall down. I fall down now, never will I get up. So I walk.

Next day, the kitchen girl give me extra rice again. Also, she says, she has special treat for me later; and at night she come to the building where I sleep and says, "Come with me."

You don't say no to the Khmer Rouge, even Khmer Rouge girl; they have gun, they can kill if they want, so I go with her to the building where the women live. She make me lie down on her mat, and she says to hug her. She's older than me, like my big sister, but she's Khmer Rouge, so I let her kiss me. Then she handle me. She does thing to me, thing I don't know before. I don't know if my body can do this thing that she want. So I hold very still, and in my mind I go somewhere else.

When she finish she gives me a lump of sugar. Like treasure, this sugar, like gold, like sapphire.

I take it and sneak over to the building where Mek sleep. I hold this sugar in the air and drop it on his chest. When he wake up, I tell him that the spirit, the one with the sugar, finally has come. We break this treasure in two and eat it very, very slow, melting on our tongue. Then I lie down next to Mek. We sleep close, like father and son, until the morning, and I sneak back to my building.

Tonight I'm lucky. Again I'm cook. I can sneak some extra rice. And this time, save it for myself.

A Khmer Rouge, he comes to the kitchen with something sticking on the end of his bayonet. He puts it on the plate and says, "Here, fry this for me."

I know what this is. It's liver. Human liver. From someone just killed. Still bouncing on the plate.

I do what he says. I do this. I cook it. I fry this human flesh.

We live here a very long time now, more than one year, on only rice soup. No meat, no fish, no spice. A body with no meat for one year has a big belly full of nothing, skin like lizard, gums all black. And this thing in the frying pan, it smell good. So good I want to eat it. I want to eat this meat. I want to. I am so hungry and it smell so good.

But I don't do it. Because maybe next time another kitchen boy, he will be eating me.

I sneak to Mek's building that night to tell him about this thing that happen in the kitchen, but I hurry so much, I crack the branch in the wood. A Khmer Rouge guarding the rice, he yells stop. "Traitor," he says. "Come out and show your face."

This is death. To be out alone at night is death. To run, that's also death. So I raise my hands and come out of the wood.

The Khmer Rouge, he click his gun, ready to fire. "You the khim player?"

I nod.

He put the gun away. "Go back to bed," he says.

• • •

The big dancer with the flag, his name is Siv. Since I been sneaking him food, he tries very hard to remember about not covering my face, but still sometime he forget. Always he says next time he will remember. This guy, he smile a little, like embarrass. A long time since I see someone smile, and I think maybe I should warn him: Khmer Rouge see you smile, they can kill you. But this guy, so kind, so simple, I think he can't hide his feeling.

He's a big guy, but each day I see him getting smaller from all this hard work and not enough food. One time at practice, he falls down and also the flag goes down. The Khmer Rouge guarding us, he gets very angry, says Siv has to come with him to talk about his bad character.

You can see in Siv's face fear, because now we all know, from the boy with malaria, what will happen. We never will see Siv again.

I tell the guard it was my fault. I say, "I trip him, I guess." I don't know why I say this, but I don't feel afraid. I feel like I have to protect this big clumsy guy who trip on his feet, this kid who always try not to cover my face with the flag.

The guard, he doesn't like this. I think he knows that maybe I'm not telling the truth. He makes a mad face, but he says, "Okay, get back to work."

And I know then I have power. Power from playing

the khim and leading the other singer. Power from also being a dancer. Power from being a little bit a star in the show. I feel big with this power—tall, not like little kid— like right now I just stop Siv from probably dying. No one here talks back to the Khmer Rouge, no one challenge them. But maybe I can now.

CHAPTER SIX

BAD HARVEST THIS TIME. THE SOIL, IT'S WORKING TOO HARD, planted too many times with no time to rest, and so the rice crop is small. But Khmer Rouge say it's because of lazy workers. So our food now is even less. The rice soup, it's like water, only gray, grit and little stone sometimes at the bottom. Some day no soup at all.

These kid working here, I know them now for almost two year. In two year they not growing bigger, taller. They only growing old.

All have bellies swole up, like balloon. All have knee and elbow big like melon. Some with hair turned yellow. Some with hair falling out. Some with fingernails scooped out like spoon. All these kid so hungry, but sometime they not able even to eat. No craving for food anymore, no energy for it.

I only can steal chaff now. It's not real food. It's the skin of the rice, what left behind after threshing. Humans can't eat this stuff. Only pigs. For humans it's too hard. Makes your shit turn to rock. But at least you shit something.

New schedule announced at meeting tonight. Work from 1 a.m. to 7 a.m., 7:30 a.m. to 1 p.m., 1:30 p.m. to 7 p.m., 7:30 p.m. to 11 p.m. Now, day and night, the same thing.

Also the word *sleep*, it's not allowed anymore. Okay to say *rest*, but not *sleep*. Forget this word.

Many night, the kitchen girl, she come for me and make me sleep in her building. I say we both can be kill if anyone finds out. She just says she can kill me herself if she want to.

When she finish with me, she gives me sugar ball or sometimes rice, but it in my mouth it's like dust. Always I save the rice for Siv or Kha. I give it when they're sleeping, put it on the mat near their head. I push them a little to wake up, then hide where they can't see. They see this food and eat it like in a dream. But never do they look around to see where it come from. Because they know that if I'm the one who give it, then maybe one night at confession meeting they have to tell.

The sugar I give always to Mek. Sometime I save it. Save it for some night when I can't sleep, so much kid moaning and crying and smelling like diarrhea. That night I get up, go see Mek. Now that I'm a little bit famous, the guards see me, they don't say anything.

If Mek sleeping, I drop this bit of sugar on his head, or maybe on his chest, so he will wake up with this good surprise. Always he think it's a stone falling down. Then he bite it and smile. Those night, we sleep together, like father and son, very safe. Only good thing in this camp, those nights I go see him.

One night, so much misery in my building, I go see Mek, but I have no treat to give. No corn, no sugar. Small stone instead, I drop it on his chest. He wake up; now he's expecting sugar and he bite it. He can't believe it, this trick! He give me fake spanking, smiling very big, then he says, this time, he has a treat for me.

We lie down; and very, very quiet he hum me old song, song illegal now in Year Zero. Old Cambodian love song, but also the Beatle, also American song. No word, this small humming in his throat, like purr, like Mek is giant cat. And me, I burrow to his side like I am the small cat.

• • •

Music practice now three time a day. And sometime even in the middle of the night. We know all the song now, very good. So every time they say practice, we know it's time for killing. We play fast, no stopping, to cover the sound of the killing, but you hear it anyhow. Sickening sound. Skull cracking. You hear it every day. Death is every day.

Real audience tonight. Not just microphone. Some high-ranking Khmer Rouge watching. Their faces orange from firelight. Like gourd. Fat and round face. Not skull face like kids. Face fat from eating good foods, like meat, like fish, like sugar.

One face I see in the crowd is tiny, like mouse. And eyes that seem like they know me. When the show is over, the little mouse girl, she comes to me. "Arn," she says. She has the voice of my little sister, but like ghost. "Arn, it's me, Sophea."

This girl, the sister could climb a tree and swear, now she's like old woman—thin hair, skin hanging off, teeth missing.

"Back at the old camp, we hear about you singing," she says. "So our aunt tells me, 'Go see Arn; maybe he has some food for us.'"

The old camp is very far. Two days walking. And the Khmer Rouge have patrol all over. I don't know how my sister can do this walk. I tell her to wait and I go see the Khmer Rouge girl who like me. I beg for food, tell her she can do anything to me if I can have some food.

My sister asleep on the grass when I get back. Asleep like almost dead. I give her three corncob—one for her, one for my aunt, one for my little brother.

She give one corn back to me. "He dead," she says. "He die after you leave. He keep calling out for you. Asking for you to bring him palm sugar."

One boy who sleep near me, five-year-old boy, little kid, like my brother, he disappear at night. I don't know where, maybe looking for food. If the Khmer Rouge find out, they can kill him. Kill me, too, for not stopping him. I know this, but I'm too tire to look for him.

In the morning at 5 a.m. the wandering boy is back. He sleep like dead, like not even breathing. The Khmer Rouge say to me, "Wake him up." This boy is so little, he not even have front teeth, so I lie for him. "This boy too sick to work," I say.

The next night he disappear again. I sneak out and I find him eating grass.

"Don't do this," I tell him. "They will kill you."

He smile like he crazy, his mouth green like grass. I bring him back to bed.

The next morning, again, he sleep like dead, like ghost. I say he is sick again.

"He not sick," says the Khmer Rouge. "He lazy. Kill him."

I beg him. "No, please don't." I don't know why. You can't say "please" to the Khmer Rouge, but I do.

The next night I can't sleep. Too much kid screaming, too much kid crying and moaning. And I don't know if this is my dream or this is real. I look around for the wandering boy and he's gone.

I look for him everywhere. By the side of the hut, in the kitchen. I see a light, a small light, in the mango grove. A bad smell there, and sometimes the bodies get bloat and blow up and pop out of the ground. I'm scared of that place, scared of ghost, but I go anyway.

And I see the wandering boy. I see him crouching, holding arm of a dead guy, chewing. I don't know how long he been doing that, eating the flesh, the human flesh; but now I know why he always asleep in the morning.

The next day, the Khmer Rouge say rice is missing in the kitchen, and they accuse this boy. Today I am too tire to say please.

They tie him and hit him. He doesn't cry. He doesn't cry because he have no feelings now. He a ghost already.

I let him die. Because now I'm a ghost myself.

• • •

New job for me. Not cook. Now I go with one other kid each night to the mango grove. We walk with the prisoner. At the mango grove, me and one other boy, we take the clothes off prisoner before the killing. I don't know why we take the clothes. Maybe to use again.

The prisoner, mostly men, but sometimes also women and also children, sometime they yell at me. Sometime they beg. Most time they stay quiet.

They kneel down, and the leader in the white shorts, he hit them with the ax. Then me and the other boy, we push them into the grave.

Sometime he hit a person once and they not die, but he says, "Bury them anyway." Sometime the people swear at me from the ground.

After, I hear them in my head. I hear them all the time.

Sometime I practice music with my eyes closed. I go away then, like to heaven, it's so quiet. In that moment I escape. Like floating above the earth, like cloud. Like not even having a body, only being a sound myself. I ride the wind up and down, sunshine sparkle on me, wind tickle me, lift me higher, higher, till no thought in my head, only music.

Then I open my eyes and come back. To smell of shit. And blood. And dead bodies. And fear. Always fear.

• • •

So much pain in my stomach tonight, I can't make it all the way to the latrine. I have to stop next to the pond. I sit on my heels and wait for the shit to come, but nothing. Not water. Just pain.

I hear running now and a guy coming close, saying, "Don't shoot. Please don't shoot." This guy is coming toward me, closer and closer, running away from the Khmer Rouge. The soldier chasing this guy, they shoot at him; they shoot everywhere. It's dark and everyone wearing black, and I think maybe they can't see me. They will shoot me if they think I'm the running-away guy. They will shoot me if they can't see me. They will shoot me for no reason.

I expect it now. I expect to be kill. It's all dark, but I can see the gunshot flash white. They shoot everywhere—*bang!*—like crazy. I see the water close to me blowing up. I hear a soft sound now, a wet sound, bullet stopping in flesh. The guy run straight to me and falls down. Right on top of me.

So this dead guy, this guy on top of me, he save me.

The Khmer Rouge, they kill whatever they hate. Sometime, even, they hate each other. They suspect always that someone is no good, and so they test, they ask questions, like trick. "Do you love Angka? More than your brother? Then tell us if your brother is bad. Tell us if you see him be lazy or steal food." You say no, they kill you. They say yes, they kill your brother. Then they kill you, too.

Always, with a kind voice, they say to each other, comrade this, comrade that. One day you are comrade. The next day corpse.

New prisoner coming to the camp all the time. No hiding them anymore. Now the Khmer Rouge take them right through the square. Tie together, head low. They beat them in front of us so we can see what happen to people with bad character. Always the Khmer Rouge watch us, all the time. They watch to see if you show any emotion to the victim. You do, they kill you.

One time, a boy in my group, he see his sister come to the square. The sister see him, too. But she look away. Pretend not to know him. Because she understand he can be kill just for being her relative.

The Khmer Rouge, they hit the prisoner, one by one, with the stick while they make us watch. Now it's time for the boy sister. I hold his hand very tight, squeeze it hard. They hit her with a stick, hit the head, the shoulder, the leg, and each time I squeeze his hand so he can't cry out. She hold her head high, then quick she go down, no more life in her, and very slow, very quiet, I lead him away.

• • •

A new soldier is guarding the band now. The old one, he fell asleep one time during practice and the head guy saw. We never see that guard again.

The new guard, we all afraid of him. Even Mek. He turn pale as soon as this guy come to our building. This new guy, he's big, tall, his eyes little, like shark. And all the time watching me. Watching everyone, but looking specially at me, like he know something bad I did.

One day after practice, he tell me to wait behind. The other boy, they so scare, they can't even look at me. Siv, he look maybe like he's gonna vomit. These boy I steal food for, these boy I protect, they want to cry but can't show it. I tell them it's okay. I say, "See you later," even though we don't know if maybe we never will see each other again.

When the kid are gone, Mek, he beg this soldier, "Kill me, I'm old. But leave this boy alone." But the soldier, he just tell Mek to scram. And me, I tell Mek scram also, using almost angry voice. "Remember what I tell you," I say to him. "If you don't live, the kid in the band can't live." Then the soldier push Mek out the door.

"Kneel on the floor," he tell me. Then he tie his red-and-white-check scarf over my eyes. It's all dark now and quiet, very quiet inside this scarf where I wait to die.

"You think you pretty good, don't you?" he says.

"You think you're a good musician, right?"

No answer is the right answer for this question.

"So play," he says.

I can't see anything inside this scarf, but this guy, he hand me the bamboo stick. "Play," he says. "Let's see you play now."

I think again of the old man who taught me to play. I think of all this practice, three times a day, every day, and I know I can do this. I let the stick fall, and one ping sound, then one more, then many, many more, so fast it's like this instrument, it's playing itself.

When I finish, he pull the scarf away and tell me to go. No look on his face. He just keep watching me all the way back to the temple.

When I come to Mek building that night he look afraid, like he see a ghost. He pinch me, pull my hair to make sure I'm real boy. Then he grab me and hold me close. We go to sleep like before, like father and son; but I think in his nightmare, Mek is crying.

The next day, the other kid, they look at me like maybe I have magic. They touch my arm like maybe this magic will rub onto them; and Siv, the big, simple guy, he drop the flag and pick me up in his arm, almost crushing my bone.

• • •

Next day, I flirt a little with the kitchen girl and take one handful of rice, not even cooked, from the sack. I do this all the time now, so not even too sneaky this time, just put it in my pocket.

I see this new guard watching me across the way, very suspicious. But I make a blank face like always.

I walk past this guy, after, on the way to meeting, my hand in front so no one can see that my pocket, it's a little fat. This guy see, though. He look at me so hard with his little shark eye, I know he can see inside my pocket. He look so hard at me I think maybe just his eye can kill me. But he don't do a thing. Only watch me go by.

This new guard, his name Sombo. I ask the kitchen girl about him. She says he's the bodyguard to one of the top guy. Very fierce, two gun, one on each side, and always making a frown face. Everyone very afraid of this guy, she says. Too quiet. And always staring.

This guy, Sombo, he catch me again. This time by the tamarind tree. Not even near the music building, not near the kitchen. Wherever I go, this guy, he show up. No one else around. But this guy, he come every time. This time he see me eating the tamarind. His little shark eyes exactly on me when I chew it.

I walk right to him. "Why you not hit me?" I say.

"Why you not tell the Khmer Rouge I steal the food?"

Still he's quiet.

"The other Khmer Rouge, they find out you not report me, they beat you, maybe kill you," I say.

He only walk away. And this time, it's me just looking at him.

Now I watch this guy all the time. I see how he tap his foot when we play the music. I see also his face is like a baby. No hair on his lip. Soft cheek. This fierce guy, he's a kid. A kid four, maybe five years older than me. A lot of Khmer Rouge soldier just teenager, but this guy, he make frown face all the time so he can seem old. Quiet all the time, and watching very suspicious so he can seem fierce. But all the time, really, he's a kid.

Also never he yell at us. Never yell at Mek. Only time he use a strict voice is when we play at the meeting, when the top guys come for celebration and we play for them. But when only us kid are around, he doesn't yell, doesn't hit. I tell Mek, "This guy, Sombo, he's not like other Khmer Rouge."

Now a lot of day, Sombo, he asks me to play for him after the band practice. First couple time, Mek hide behind a building and watch to make sure nothing bad can happen. But soon he leave me alone with Sombo, no problem. I play for him now, no blindfold, only playing the song. Still no talking.

One day I ask him again why he never tell the other Khmer Rouge about me stealing the food.

"I see what you do," he says. "Sometimes you give food to the other kid. So I stay quiet."

Finally this guy talk, and I don't know what to say.

"Before the Khmer Rouge," he says, "I was orphan, and hungry all the time. The people, they judge me, shame me, hit me sometime for what I do to get food." He look over at the rice field, where kid are working now at night. "Why I would give this shame to other kid?"

So one Khmer Rouge is good, I think. One guy, this Sombo, he is good inside.

Many night now, I play the khim for Sombo. He sit under a tree after dinner and I play song. These night I can lose myself in the music because I don't sing the word. No blood-red field, no glory to Angka, only notes. No hate in notes; notes just notes. All the hate is in the word. Also this music, it's not to cover the sound of people being kill, of skull cracking. It's for this one guy, this Khmer Rouge who really is just a kid acting like tough. Like me.

One night I show him how to play the khim, like the old man taught me. His hands clumsy—hard skin from hard work—and I tell him, "Touch it light, like hummingbird wing." He hold the bamboo stick dainty now, like girl; and inside I smile at this Khmer Rouge, this tough guy, playing the music so gentle.

After, we walking home, I ask him, "The other Khmer Rouge, what make them be so bad?"

Sombo says, "It's not bad or good. They kill only so they won't be killed themself."

CHAPTER SEVEN

ONE WAY TO KNOW HOW LONG WE'VE BEEN HERE: COUNT THE season. Eight harvest now means two year and a half. The Khmer Rouge give us new black clothes two or three times a year. Just one shirt, one pant. Just one, because no one can have any possession at all. No toy, no pillow, no bowl. Not one thing.

Another way to tell the time: how often they let us wash in the pond. Maybe one time every six weeks. Sometime the clothes smell bad. Like shit and sweat. Stiff from so much wearing. But sometime you have one hour to rest, and the Khmer Rouge say, "Okay, jump in the pond." Everybody at the same time. Even the kid too weak.

When I was a small boy I like to take my clothes off for swimming. Jumping. Doing a flip. Throwing a leech at my little brother. A fun thing, too dangerous to think of now.

Here, they separate us for the bath. Girl with girl, boy with boy. But Kha, he says we can see the girls, see naked girls, if we crawl under the building where we sleep. Siv giggle and shut his eyes tight.

Me, I cover my eye but peek out between my finger. They timid, these girl, when they take off the black uniform. Nervous, I think, to show private thing, like breast, like bottom. But these girl, they not like the apsara dancer with round breast carved on temple wall. They like old woman. All bone. Skin like paper. Some with hair falling out. The boy see this, they don't want to look anymore.

When it's our turn, we play a little bit. Me and Kha and Siv, we pretend we like elephant, making water come out our nose. Not crazy splashing. Not crazy trick. Not enough energy in us to be crazy. If you crazy, you drown. So we just play gentle with the water. And maybe try to sink a little. Hold your nose and go down to the bottom, all quiet and dark. No blood smell, no loudspeaker music down there. No Khmer Rouge.

But you can't sink yourself. You go down, and you feel like you're floating again. Because nothing in your stomach.

• • •

Everyone here is afraid. Not just us kid but also the Khmer Rouge. The low-ranking soldier, always they have to praise the leader, do whatever he say, or maybe get sent away. Maybe to the manure pile, maybe the mango field.

Then one day that leader, someone says he's a traitor and now he's the one who goes to the mango grove. And after that a new guy in charge, and all the soldier, they pretend they never even know the old leader.

The Khmer Rouge, they do anything to stay alive. Same for all of us. Always trying to see which way the wind is going.

One day I see Sombo walking in the middle of camp with a new high-ranking guy. I run to him, ask where they going. The other guy, he look at me like pest and push Sombo to keep walking. Sombo, he stare at me with little shark eye, like never he even know me, and says to go away.

I pull on him, on his sleeve, and say, "Please, I want to go with you."

Then Sombo, he make an angry face, mean and ugly, and he swear at me. He spit on the dirt and call me a very bad word. Like he hate me. He push me away, hard, till I fall down on the path. And I see only his back now as he walk away with this new leader.

How sudden the wind change here, where Sombo, this one guy always so good to me, now is so mean to me.

That night I go to see Mek and tell him what happen. I say now I hate Sombo, that he trick us, that really he like all the other Khmer Rouge. But Mek only shake his head.

"All the time, Sombo save you," he says. "This time he save you again."

I can't understand.

"You don't know?" Mek says. "Sombo in trouble himself. He bring water to some guy at the manure pile, some guy still loyal to the old leader. Little kid, spy for new leader, he tells on Sombo. Now Sombo goes to jail."

"But why he calls me that bad name?"

"So you don't follow him. To save you from being punish also."

Every minute now I think only about Sombo. I worry that maybe he is in the jail, dying for water. Or that the new leader will beat him. Or maybe kill him. And every minute I try to think of how to get to the jail—the place where before there were horses, now men tied up—how to sneak there. Maybe to bring him water, maybe to help him escape.

All day I wait for a chance, then at dinner a soldier, he grab me and say he need me for a job. I know what this job is. It's like when they took the old music teacher to the mango grove; they want me to come see what they do to Sombo. I don't even feel afraid. I'm not little kid anymore. Like old man myself now.

This soldier he grab me and Siv, he take us to the temple. The temple, the place where the torture happen. In there other soldier, they have the prisoner tied up. Hand behind, head down. Quick I look for Sombo. But these prisoner all old people.

"These people, they no good," says one Khmer Rouge. "They old; they don't work so hard. They gonna die soon anyway." Then, very quick, he take the ax and hit them in the back of the head. Blood fly everywhere. The wall of the temple, beautiful tile, beautiful painting, now all dripping with blood.

Then the Khmer Rouge says to us, "It's time for your job. You pee on them. You pee on their head."

I think: I will not do this terrible thing, I will not do this.

But then I look down, and I see the urine coming out of me.

After this bad thing me and Siv, we leave the temple. We so shame of this bad thing we done, we don't even look at each other. Siv, he cries like a baby. Then he grab my arm. Coming toward us, walking through the middle of camp, it's Sombo. Like ghost, I think, but when I see him smile, I know it's really him. We run to him and he explain.

The new leader, he said Sombo was corrupt, that he should be kill. Then someone else, he said the new leader, he was corrupt himself. Lotta fighting, then all of a sudden the old leader is back in power. And he set Sombo free.

The wind, somehow, it change again.

Now Sombo is back, I play for him every night. And sometimes, after I play, he let me listen to his radio. One station is Angka speaking. It says the rice fields in Cambodia every day now full of joyful cries of the peasant working. Great harvest coming. Soon, it says, everyone in Cambodia will have dessert every day.

Here kid are starving. Here the rice plant also look like sick. The soil very tire now from planting and planting and planting with no rest. Just like the kid. Sick from working, working, working and no rest.

Another station is Voice of America. This station, we get caught listening, we die. This Voice of America, it speak Khmer and it say Vietnamese soldier are coming across the border to fight the Khmer Rouge, to take over Cambodia. It say fighting has begun many miles from here, near the border. But Sombo snap the button off before I can hear more.

I hide from Sombo that this news makes me a little bit excited. That maybe now I hope we can be rescue. Always growing up, we hear the Vietnamese, they like the devil, that they cut the ear off the people they kill. The ear, maybe also the tongue, and cook little baby for eating them. Maybe these devil soldier, I think maybe they can beat the Khmer Rouge. But when I go to bed, I also feel afraid. Afraid that maybe these Vietnamese, they will kill us kid, too. For helping the Khmer Rouge.

All the time I get a little more famous here. The other kid, Kha and Siv, they play the music or they dance; but me, I'm the only one who play the song, sing, dance, do everything, always with big smile on my face. So now, the leader in the white shorts, he notice me. He says to come to his house to play music. No others, only the khim player, he says.

Kha and Siv, they all make a worried face. Mek, he make a sound like choking. But I don't feel afraid. I feel hype, excited now, because maybe I can get food for myself, for Kha, for Siv, for Mek. So maybe all of us, we can live one more day, then one day more, until maybe the Vietnamese will come and kill this guy.

This leader, his house not at the camp. Down the path where we first came to this temple, in the town. But the town is not a town anymore. The houses all empty, with vine growing over top, roof all sunk in, and weed inside. The streets empty, too; car and bike stop right in the middle, also suitcase, sleeping mat, even sewing machine, all drop in the middle of the road by people leaving in a hurry. No people, no cat or dog, even. Only dust blowing.

Ghost town, except for this guy's house. Biggest house in town. Yellow, with iron gate. And big porch where I play the khim. Inside is the party. Many, many girl and only this guy and a few other. But the leader, the guy in white, he doesn't care about the music. Only girls and the alcohol from France call Hennessy. He smoke many cigarette in one night and has many girl with him. Khmer Rouge girl, mostly, but also girl from the camp, skinny girl, young, and very afraid, crying, shame face afterward.

I play so long, same song over and over, I almost fall asleep playing. Finally the head guy, he come to me and says to stop. I pack up my instrument, but he says no, tonight you sleep here. This party goes for three days, maybe, and I see this guy bring many girl to his room, also sometimes boy. Many time each night I get up and go sleep in a different place so he never can find me.

When finally I go back to camp, I have some good food to share with Siv and Kha. One special thing I steal: sweet potato. Siv and Kha and me, we eat this not cooked and hurry to swallow so no one can see. Next day when we shit, you can see it. Orange pieces in our shit. We kick dirt on it to hide it. Because the Khmer Rouge, they always watching to see who steal food. They even look at our shit.

The head guy, he treat me a little bit special now. Not like other kid, bringing them to his room. Like helper. Like assistant. I don't know why he treat me good like this, and always I think maybe sometime he gonna make me come to his room, but instead he treat me like toy, like pet. I play for him and he give me good food, like tiny bit fish and vegetable sometimes. Also he has a little white horse, and one day he says I can ride it. I think maybe it's a trick, to see if maybe I will run away; but he says I can ride this horse to another camp, give the head guy there a letter.

This horse, he goes fast, like flying. I hold the mane, no saddle or anything, so I just feel him under me, hoof galloping. I see up ahead small river, like stream, and I think: oh God, we can't go, but this horse, he fly right over and keep going.

Strange thing is happening now. Nice thing. But very strange. Smile is on my face. Not fake smile like when we sing song about Angka, but real smile, and laughing. Also wetness on my cheek like rain, but it's tear. For three year laughing not allowed, crying not allowed. Now, on this horse, I am laughing so much I am also crying.

This camp where I bring the letter is big, a lot bigger than ours, huge, and for men only. Like a city of one hundred rice field with one thousand men working. All around are ditch for holding water. Long, straight row, like river. And field also huge, with many, many men digging in the mud. The whole place one giant farm.

The leader at this camp, he has one wristwatch on each arm, canteen across the chest, and grenade on each hip. He hold the letter I give him a little while, then yell to an old guy sweeping the floor. "Old man," he says. "Come here."

The old guy, very slow, like grandfather, come over and squint at the letter. Word by word, he read it to the head guy. When he's done, the head guy smack him on the ear and call him stupid old man. Then he says to me, "This guy was professor at college, now my slave. He so slow, some day I think I might kill him. But then who would read my letter?" He smiles wide, his gums black, like dog's. "A few of these people who can read, we have to keep them around, right, comrade?"

I don't know why he ask me this. Why he talks to me so friendly. Then I understand. I come on a horse, with letter from high-ranking Khmer Rouge: he thinks I'm young comrade, young Khmer Rouge.

Back on the horse now, I make him go slow. Slow so I don't have to go back too soon. No one watching me now. No one around at all. First time in three year, except for the manure pile, I ever been alone.

I think about the leader with black gum, how he thought I was Khmer Rouge. I think also about how everyone wearing black pajamas now, everyone in the whole country dress the same. No way to know who is Khmer Rouge and who is just citizen. And I have the idea to maybe stay on this horse. Anyone try to stop me, I say I'm Khmer Rouge bringing important letter. Then maybe I can ride and ride and never go back to the camp where I see all those killing. No more smell of blood and dead body, no more kid moaning at night, no more living every minute like maybe you can get kill for no reason. Maybe I can live in the jungle, go fishing for food, and ride and ride and ride until I get somewhere else, somewhere where no Khmer Rouge anymore.

Then I think about Mek. And Siv and Kha and even Sombo. All of them will worry. They will think maybe I disappear like all those kid in the mango grove. I think also about what will happen to the band if I leave. One other problem: where a kid like me can go? No home exist anymore. My family all scatter at different camps or dead. No way to find them. Also, I never before been anywhere except my town and the camp.

I wish I can be like this horse. Like simply animal. Only eating, sleeping, running.

We been walking very slow, but now we at the stream we cross last time, when the horse, he flew over. And the horse, now he pull to get going. I hug his neck and whisper in his ear, "What we should do?" He snort a little, then plod his feet very slow through the stream toward home. He know only one thing: how to get back to the camp. Me, I guess I'm like this horse after all.

For a few day I live at the leader's house. Play music a little, but mostly I take care of the horse. Any time the leader, he need a message to deliver or maybe to bring thing to his house, like cigar, like Hennessy, I ride the horse and bring it. I ride to the camp sometime, see Siv and Kha, Mek and Sombo, show them how fast this horse can go, also to sneak them some good food from the leader house.

Me and this horse, we friend now; we fly over the field and race very fast, no one watching. Rest of the time I just take care of him, give him water, scratch between his ear so much he go to sleep standing up.

Even okay if I sleep sometime. Even if it's daytime.

And now I sleep very deep, like never before in the building with all the kid crying and moaning. I sleep good here, in the straw with the horse, his good smell, his breath very sweet and warm on me. Now I sleep like thirsty man getting water for the first time; never can I get enough of this good sleep.

And sometime I think maybe it's okay if the Vietnamese never come, never rescue us.

CHAPTER EIGHT

NO MORE TIME FOR SLEEPING NOW. THE RADIO, IT SAYS THE
Vietnamese are coming close. Now is panic; everyone flee
the leader house, jump in truck and ride away very fast.
One guy, he take the little white horse and ride away.
They don't even remember me, so I have to run all the
way to camp by myself.

Panic is at the camp, too; some kid running around
like crazy, some crying, a few running into the wood. But
no one chase them. All the Khmer Rouge soldier in the
middle of the square, polishing the gun, loading string of
bullet onto their chest, canteen, grenade, knife, anything
they can use to kill.

The kid who not escape, they all in a line, each one getting a rifle. Some kids so little, the gun is taller than them. Other kid, bigger one, they play with the gun like toy. One little boy, he looks down inside the hole where the bullet is, and—*bang!*—he shoot himself in the head, die right there; no one even notice.

Chaos everywhere, but I see Siv and Kha strapping the string of bullet on themself. I run to them, say, "Follow me," and the three of us, we go to find Sombo. "Please," we beg him. "Let us come with you." We tell him we can be good fighter—run fast, hide, shoot, do anything. Sombo pull me away to talk private. He look at me hard.

"Why you not run away?" he says. "You leave now, maybe no one will see you. Maybe you go home now, find your family."

Family. How can I find my family? My family now is only these two guys, Siv and Kha. And Mek. And also maybe Sombo, this Khmer Rouge, this one guy always kind to me. I don't say this to him. Also I don't tell him now I'm more scared of Vietnamese than even Khmer Rouge. I just say, "I show you how to play the khim. Now you show me how to use the gun."

All the kid from the band, from the dance group, about twenty kid, the Khmer Rouge put us in special fighting group with Sombo as leader. Kid only. Little Fish with the Big Sting they call us. Special mission for our group. Spy. Sneak in place where the men can't go. Bring back information. Big honor to be in this group, they tell us.

All of a sudden I'm Khmer Rouge. These people I hate, now I'm one.

Strange feeling, but also a little bit good. Like now we have some power, now we have gun, now we all Cambodian fighting together to kill the Vietnamese.

I think of all the time I play soldier with my little brother, how we hold our arms like airplane, how we shoot with our fingers. Little part of my heart is afraid now. But most of me, I feel excited. Real war is happening now. And I am real soldier.

Our group, the Little Fish, we the first to leave camp. But Mek, he has to stay, to fight in a different group with the men. He come to our group, his face very sad. Slow, he touch the gun on my shoulder, the bullet on my chest. Then he bless me, sprinkle dirt on my head to protect me and chant, very low, very quiet. Old Buddhist chant from before the Khmer Rouge. He chant a long time, tear running down, then he open his eye, kiss me on the forehead.

"All my children die," he says. "Now, you my son. And I think maybe now because this war, we never will see each other again."

I tell him no. I tell him when all this fighting is over,

we will be together again, again like father and son, eating sugar, singing the old songs; but he only shake his head.

The ground now is shaking, same as long time ago when my brother and I play war outside the movie palace. I know this sound. It means war is coming, coming close. I look to Mek to say good-bye; but now his eyes have no light, like before, like when I met him, dead inside. And I know already in his heart he said good-bye to me. Already in his heart, like his children, I'm gone.

The first time I shoot the gun, it kill me. Big gun, tall as me, I put it on my shoulder and aim at the palm tree. Just for test. Just to see what it feels. The trigger is like old hinge, stiff, not moving, then—*bang*! In my shoulder a hard fist—very strong, like fist of a giant—hit me, lift me off my feet, and now I'm flying in the air, no sound, only dirt spraying. Very slow I float, looking up, high; the sky very beautiful, blue, and cloud like pillow.

I'm on my back now, very peaceful. And I think: this must be what dying is. Very nice feeling. No pain. No sound. Not even feeling like I have a body.

Then I see Siv leaning over me with a worried face. Maybe Siv in heaven, too, I think. He talking, moving his lip, but only sound now is like Sombo radio when he can't find the station. Rushing sound. Like strong river is nearby.

Now I see Kha and also other boy, all laughing. I see this laughing, but no sound with it. Then Sombo come and lean over me. I ask him if I'm dead. My own voice, very big in my head.

Sombo smile, shake his head. "You okay," he says. He is yelling very hard, I can tell from his face, but his voice very tiny and very far. "Your ear, too, it will be okay," he says.

Rest of the day, all the boy try shooting the guns. Nobody train us. We just teach ourself. Some fall down like me; some, the big one, they don't. All of us, we can't hear after. And we shout at each other and point, make a face so we can understand, laughing when no one can hear. Laughing more when someone falls down. We shoot and shoot, killing only the grass, the trees. So much fun to have a real gun. Sort of like pretend time with my brother. Only better.

We walk a very long time now to get to the war. We carry gun, bullet, grenade, pot for cooking, all kinda thing. All boy, only one girl, little girl with missing tooth in front, she carry the rice. Big bag of rice, she carry on her head. Long walk, three day, very hot, gun is heavy, very long, hurt the shoulder to carry. Big guy like Siv, even hard for him to carry. Little guy like me, sometime I drag it behind.

Sombo shout at me very angry. "This gun is your life. You lose it, mean you give it to the enemy."

He also yell at Kha for walking too slow. "You don't keep up, we leave you behind," he says, even though Kha have diarrhea very bad now, so bad he has to run to the bush all the time.

This Sombo is a different guy. Not the same guy who plays the khim very dainty, like girl. This Sombo, he's real tough guy now.

Our group, the Little Fish, we meet up now with big group of real soldier. We hold our gun very proud, make ourself tall, face fierce, so we also can be tough guy. But these soldier, so busy digging ditch for fighting, they don't pay attention.

That night, their leader, short guy with a Buddha belly, he says our unit has important job. Like a hiding game. He says we only have to sneak into the field, tall grass, perfect for hiding, he says, and sniff with our nose. "The Vietnamese, they have special smell, bad smell, from bad food they eat," he says. "You smell them, you can tell us where they hide."

One kid, dancer from the old camp, he asks what we do if they see us.

"You shoot the air," the leader says. "Then we know where you are, we come and help you."

Our group, now we're very scared but also very excited. Important job to do and real soldier for backup. Also this leader says he has a special herb to protect us. "Make you feel extra brave," he says. "Make the bullet bounce off you."

This herb, he says, just extra protection. "Little fish like you, smaller than regular soldier, too hard to see, too hard to hit," he says. "No bullet can find a little fish."

With only a sliver moon for light, we crawl through the tall grass like snake, not talking, only sound is heart thumping in our belly. We go far across this open field, like cobra, very fierce, very brave, no grown-up to tell us where to go. Only our nose for guide.

Then we smell it. Bad smell, sour, like cabbage cooking. Vietnamese smell, and also strange language. A language very fast, very angry. We stop now, so close to these soldier, not knowing what to do. The dancer, he whisper at me, says, "Let's go back." Another kid, this kid very short, shorter than me, he says maybe he can stand up, see what the Vietnamese look like, see if really the bad smell is babies cooking. I try to grab his leg but too late. He stands up only one minute, then the bullets come.

Now is panic everywhere in our group. The standing-up kid, he turn like a statue, not moving. Another kid, he jump out of our hiding place and run back where we came. Another kid, he only hug himself in the grass and cry.

Then the standing-up boy, he sink down in the dirt, only a dull sound of bullet going into his flesh. The running boy, we can hear him now, lying in the grass behind us, crying, saying only the word *mommy*, over and over. The rest of us, we don't remember even that we have gun. We just make ourself very small, very low, like worm, like invisible, and wait for the real soldiers to come rescue us.

Now bullets also coming from behind. Real soldiers, finally, they shooting at Vietnamese and coming to save us. But some kid so scared, they go crazy; they try to escape, they run from these new bullets from behind, run to the Vietnamese side to get away. They got shot in front from Vietnamese, in back from Khmer Rouge.

After, only six Little Fish survive. Me and Siv and Kha and three others, we huddle back at the camp, our bone chattering, waiting for the Khmer Rouge to tell us "good job." But they don't pay attention; they only want to talk to themself or maybe sleep. Later, the head guy, he walk past our group; now everyone asleep but me. "These little fish, we got to get more of them," he says to another guy. "They good for catching the big fish."

I think about, long time ago, catching frog with Hong, how you put little frog on the string and wait for the big one to come eat him. And I understand now. We not real soldiers. We just bait.

One day after fighting Sombo tells me to come with him. No big deal. Kha and Siv, they know I'm a little bit Sombo favorite, so they just close their eye to nap. When me and Sombo, we get to the edge of camp, I see group of kid. Little girl who carries the rice and other kid I never saw before. Sombo says we leaving this camp now to become a new group. I ask what about Kha and Siv, but Sombo, he doesn't say anything. He says only march, and he keep his shark eyes on me so I don't look back.

Like brother to me, Siv and Kha, And not even a chance to say good-bye.

Many day walking, through rice fields and also forest, hottest time of the year, no rain, the sun like fire on our skin. Our leg like wood, our mouth like dust. All of us carry a heavy gun; but the girl who carry the rice on her head, she also has a hard job and is just little kid. Sometime her knee wobble under this heavy load, and sometime I carry the sack for her. Always this girl walk behind me now. "You have like magic power," she tell me one time. "All this shooting and never do you get hurt. So I stay near you and maybe nothing bad will happen to me."

Finally, after two day walking, we get to the new camp. New job now for the Little Fish. We stay in trench, deep trench, near the road, wait for Vietnamese to come. We hear them coming, we jump out and shoot. Like before, real soldier stay behind. Little Fish go out front.

We dig this trench ourself, then hide there, take turn sleeping. But three boy in my trench, all of us, we too scared to sleep. One boy, he sings very quiet, a baby song, like lullaby, a song for learning the numbers, over and over. The other boy, he pick small bugs from his hair and eat. I lie in this trench and think: maybe this is my grave.

All night is very quiet. Only maybe some cricket. Then you hear it. Bird screeching very loud. Next you feel it. Earth shivering. Because tanks are coming. Bird is the first warning. Bird knows to fly away from this fight coming.

Because Vietnamese, they have tank, cannon, many soldier, and rifle that shoots one hundred bullets with no stopping. We just kid with old gun. Shoot only one bullet each time.

Never before I been so afraid. At the camp you afraid all the time, because any time you can die. From starving, from diarrhea, from ax. But I learn a way to stay alive there. I learn to play my music, do what the Khmer Rouge say, never make them mad. And somehow—some good luck, some good thinking, also maybe some good trick—I stay alive.

Now no good thinking, no good trick can help. And I think: why I stayed alive? Only so I can die today?

We jump out of the trench and into so many bullet it's like rain. But we too scared to shoot, only hide in the grass. Then I feel wetness on my cheek, something warm. I touch; and on my hand is blood. I look at the singing boy and see that half of his face now missing; and all on my neck, in my hair, is blood and brain and tiny piece of bone.

The other boy, he vomit. But me, I feel crazy, like all of a sudden my blood is electric; and I shoot and shoot and shoot. Only shooting, no thinking. No fear, even. You don't even see what you shooting. Except one time, I see this Vietnamese guy, kid, like teenage, running to hide behind a tree, and I point the gun at him and shoot. He stop, his face surprise, like almost smiling. Then he gone. Only grass where he was. Standing one minute, gone next minute. Dead. I think: this guy is dead. And I'm the one who do it. I feel crazy, like not myself, like shooting machine. Like maybe I can shoot and shoot forever.

Until Sombo, he tell me, "Okay, stop now, it's all over." And he take me back to camp, where right away I go to sleep, very hard, like dead myself.

• • •

More walking, more hiding, until we get to another camp. We join now with other kid, some real Khmer Rouge, and some like us, just kid who get gun one week ago to fight the Vietnamese.

We now one unit. But one Khmer Rouge, young guy name Phat, maybe only one or two years older, he says the new kids are not real Khmer Rouge. Not loyal from the beginning like him. We only soldier now because they force us.

So Phat, he says new job will prove if the Little Fish really love Angka. When tank comes, he says, we have to climb up and put the grenade inside. Very, very dangerous this job.

Little girl who carry the rice, who now cuddle at my side at night to be warm, tells me don't do it, it suicide. But I tell her it's also suicide to say no. Because this guy, I think he might kill us if we don't.

So next time a tank comes, me and one other boy, we run to it and climb on like monkey. The other boy, he slip off the top, and I don't see him anymore. I hang on, tank still moving, like big angry animal underneath me. I turn the handle, open the top, and drop the grenade inside. Then jump off and run back to the woods very fast.

Big noise, then the tank goes in direction like crazy, crash into trees.

Again I feel this electricity in me. Like I have a power bigger than me. Like even if I do crazy thing, I can't be kill. Then I look back and see the other boy sitting in the middle of the road, his leg not right, too short, with bone sticking out, jagged, white, and blood gushing. He points to something a little bit nearby, something on the road where the tank just pass by. His foot.

After this big fight, we get a new gun. Like Vietnamese gun, this one shoot many bullets no stopping, automatic, just touch the trigger. Lighter also, this gun, and smaller. Good for kids like us.

But no one show us how to use it. They just give it and leave. And one boy, kid from dance group, he just playing around. All of a sudden the gun shoot itself; and this boy has blood on him, and thing from inside, like liver, intestine, now outside, spilling out. He try to catch it with his hand; but all these bloody thing, slippery, keep spilling out.

I go over and hold this boy, rock him like a baby, and also hum a song from my aunt, a song for falling asleep, until his body turn cold, his face like wax, no life in him anymore.

I stand up, see myself cover in blood—so dark, almost black, like ink. I think maybe I should wash it, get rid of it. But I think maybe it can protect me, this boy's blood on my body, so I paint myself with it—wipe it on my face, my throat, my arms. I take his gun also and strap it across my chest, two guns on me now.

I go see Phat, the Khmer Rouge boy who say I'm not real soldier. So he can see what I am now.

CHAPTER NINE

SOMBO NOW IS VERY STRICT. NO MORE TIME FOR HIM AND ME to sit together and talk or listen to the radio. Always gruff face, always short temper. And I think maybe now this guy, this only friend I have, he doesn't like me anymore.

I see some kid give up. Just slip behind and never seen again. Other kid, I see them shoot themself, I think on purpose. One kid, he go crazy and run straight into bullets. And sometime I think maybe I will give up, too. Or run away. My family, probably everyone is dead. My friend Siv, Kha, Mek, I probably never will see them again. If Sombo, the only person I know in the whole world, he doesn't care about me anymore, then why I keep going?

I look at him now, across the fire, soup cooking in the middle, his face hard, like different person from the guy who let me steal food, guy who I teach to play the khim, and think maybe he won't care, maybe not even notice, if I disappear.

Soup is almost ready. First time in three day we kid have a meal, and everyone lean close to the pot and smell it—rice girl on one side of me, and Phat, the Khmer Rouge kid who hate me, on the other side. Then, from nowhere, we hear the whistle that says a bomb—from Vietnamese cannon—is coming this way. Sombo, he reach across the fire and grab me, throw me on the ground. The shell land right in the pot and metal and soup and dirt fly everywhere.

After, I look up from the ground and see Phat, the kid next to me, piece of him hanging from the tree, piece of him on the ground. And I wonder: why Sombo save me but let this other kid die?

Big battle that night, many kid die. Kid run right in front of me, get killed. You think you never can get used to a thing this sad, kid dying, but you do. You think maybe you want to die also. But you don't.

You not living. And you not dead. You living dead.

The Angka voice on Sombo radio now says we have to walk north. And so after many days walking one direction, now we go the other. Same field we saw before. Same place where we fight the Vietnamese and so many kid die. The radio says Vietnamese now gone from here, but I think I still can smell their bad smell in the air.

Walking very quiet now. In case maybe they still around. No sound. Not even breathing. Then the little rice girl, she step on stick or something in the ground, something that make a click. Right away Sombo yell at her, "Don't move!"

But this little girl, she so scare by Sombo yelling, she shy back from him and turn to me, then—*pop!*—a puff of smoke where she was standing.

After, her leg is gone. She cries very hard, scream for her mother, until she faint from pain.

Sombo tell us the Vietnamese do this, bury small bomb in the ground, called land mine. You step on it, you can lose your leg; you touch it, you lose your hand. A coward weapon, he says, for scaring us, for making us afraid every step.

This weapon, this land mine, it means now that even the earth is our enemy.

Some kid in our group, they grumble now. They say Sombo is no good. They say too many kid getting kill. And one guy, he look at me and say, "It's your fault Phat get kill." Another one, he point at me. "You," he says. "You Sombo's favorite."

Then Sombo come by and yell at me, say I have to carry the rice sack and my gun from now on.

The other kid smirk, but I understand now why Sombo so gruff to me. Like before, like back at the camp, he protecting me.

We carry the little rice girl, take turn, her leg tied in a rag where used to be her knee. Now we go even slower. Too hard to walk and carry this girl. And too scare to even put our foot down on the path.

Bad smell now coming from her leg, all swole and turn black. She very sweaty, too, and panic, even when she sleeping; she toss and turn and cry from the pain. All of a sudden she grab me in the night, call me Mama, and say, "Please, please, stop this pain." Then she die. And finally, for her, no more pain.

We hike to camp to get a new rice girl, but only get a skinny boy, smaller than the girl, too little even to carry a gun, kid name Koong. How this kid can carry rice sack, I ask Sombo. This kid, Sombo tell us, has special job. This kid special trained to catch rat, insect, frog, snake, anything we can eat. Beside, he tell us, hardly any rice left in our sack.

Many more days walking, and I think sometimes we go one way, next time the other. Like maybe we don't know where we are. Many rice field now are all weed. Some with big hole where the Vietnamese shoot the cannon. Village now are only building, no people, all cover with weed, with vine.

But one place we stop looks like a place I been before. Small pond, full of frog, near the train track. I know this place. This the place where I come with Hong for frogging. Long time ago. Before I ever hear of the Khmer Rouge. Back when I was a kid.

Sometime when we wander around in the wood, we see other platoon, like ours, small, sometime kid only, sometime regular soldiers. And always one girl with them to carry the rice. One time our group, we pass another group resting in the forest. This group, real Khmer Rouge, very high ranking, has one little rice girl—tiny, hair almost turn white like old woman. We walk by, and this girl whisper my name. How she know me, I wonder.

She say my name again, and I know now this is my sister. My little sister, Sophea, ten year old, now like tiny old woman, bent over from carrying the rice sack.

Too dangerous to show that we are family. And so I pass by, giving her only one small nod of the head. Then

I say to Sombo that I'm too tired to keep walking—I don't care now about the other kid saying I'm Sombo's favorite—and Sombo, he says okay.

When night comes, I go to my sister. She touch my face and whisper how she love me. Her lips crack from no food, no water; they touch my ear and it feel like butterfly wing, like angel, like heaven. She pinch me, too, and say I'm too skinny. I don't know what I look like anymore; but I look at this tiny girl, crooked back, knee swole from not enough food, belly full of air, and I think she is the most beautiful thing I ever see in my lifetime.

When morning come and it time to go, she touch my face. "Don't be too brave, Arn," she says. "You hide from the bullet so I can see you again. Okay?"

Long time ago I kill all hope in myself. And live only like animal, survive one day, then one day more. Now here is my little sister. My family. Someone who love me. Alive. And I say, "Now I know you are still living, I will live, too."

CHAPTER TEN

SOMBO SNEAK AWAY NOW TO LISTEN TO HIS RADIO. BUT I SNEAK behind and hear two thing.

Voice of Angka says glorious victory is coming soon. Vietnamese now are running away in shame and defeat. Angka says Khmer Rouge fighters cut off the ear, cut out the tongue, eat the liver of dead Vietnamese, get stronger every day.

Voice of America says Vietnamese now in control of the eastern province, taking more land every day. Also that many people from Cambodia fleeing to Thailand.

I don't know what is truth. But I keep in my mind this place, this Thailand.

• • •

Hiding in the trench tonight, we can see smoke from bomb each time getting closer. Big open field between us and the Vietnamese; but their cannon can shoot everywhere, this way and that, trying to find us. Each time a bomb land, Sombo, he turn his head in that direction and count, only his lip moving, like he can do a math that tells where the next one will land.

All of a sudden he pick me up out of the trench and tell me to run. I do like he says; but a big burst of wind, like the hand of a giant, it push me in the back, shove me on the ground. For one second the air all around is hot, thick, sucking my inside out—my lung, my ear, even my eye, they feel like they coming out of my head. Then the whole world explode, everything flying—dirt, tree, rock, everything in the air. And me, I fly, too. And I think: oh, my sister, I'm sorry; I can't see you again because now I'm dying.

When I wake up, now in a different place, my whole body is sore. I touch my leg, my arm, my head, and each part still there. Inside of my head is thick, like mud, but I can hear a voice telling me to drink a little water. It's Sombo, his canteen to my mouth.

I drink a little and ask him, "Why you save me again?"

He frown a little. "You have to live to see your sister."

Now I frown. "How you know about my sister?"

"All the time I'm watching you," he says. "All the time."

I don't say it to Sombo, but all the time I watch him, too.

One day walking over a hill we look down and see a strange thing. A village like before the Khmer Rouge. People living in the house, family, working in the field. Even chicken in the yard. Like toy, this village, so pretty.

Maybe the war is over now. Maybe we been in the wood so long we don't know it. Maybe we can go this village and have real food: chicken, maybe also vegetable, maybe fish stew even. Then I see some Vietnamese soldier walking through the village, calling out to the people. "All people," he says. "War is over, come to the center of village for free rice. Gift from your new Vietnamese ruler."

All the villager, we see them run to the soldier, open hand for food, basket, can, anything they can fill. I see one old lady fall down, then hear the gunshot that kill her. Then many gunshot. Sombo yell at us to shoot, too, to shoot down at the Vietnamese from our spot on the hill. And now everyone is shooting at the toy village, until finally it is only smoke and fire and dead body.

After, Sombo make us walk through the village to

make sure no one is left. I do what he says, but each time, I turn the body over and look at the face. I know they don't live in this village, this place so far from my town; I know I won't find them, but each time I think maybe I will see my family.

One woman I find not dead. She's lying on the ground, her body like cut in half, legs not attach to her body and blood, blood everywhere. She sit up, like all of a sudden she has strength, like cobra, and she spit at me. "You Khmer Rouge," she says. "I hate you."

I think for one second maybe she mean somebody else.

"You!" she says again. She mean me—me, I'm Khmer Rouge.

Then she start to cry. "Please," she says. "Kill me." She grab my ankle and beg. "Don't let me die like this. Please shoot me."

And I look at this woman, pretty face, long braid, dying slow in the hot sun; and I do it. I shoot her.

At night many things to be afraid of.

Leech, they glow white; they crawl in the soil, then jump on your body, your leg, your private part, your back, all time sucking the blood from you.

Small noise, gecko calling, stick breaking, any small noise can mean Vietnamese are close.

Snake, tiger, poison frog, all these thing can come in the night, kill you no noise at all.

Now I have one more thing to be afraid. Now, if finally I can go to sleep, I dream of the woman who spit at me and call me Khmer Rouge. Now, in my dream, I feel her finger, cold, only bone, but strong like a giant, pulling me down into the grave with her.

A few days later, another big battle. Our soldiers, they run in every direction, scatter like rat. Too much tank, too much cannon from the Vietnamese, and so everyone run and get separate. Our group, now only seven kid plus Sombo and Koong, the little ratcatcher boy, is walking again—walking, walking, always walking, not knowing where we go, just walking.

We walk so much we walk sleeping. Big guy in front of me, I hold on to him, grab his shirt, so I don't get lost or maybe fall down asleep. He try to shake me off, but I hang on him for my life.

We carry gun, bullet, grenade, many thing for fighting; but also we carry food and water, pot for cooking, also other thing. Heavy thing. So heavy now we drop thing, one small thing first, then more, then more, till we have only the gun and bullet, no food, no water. After this so thirsty, but no water to drink, so we drink the urine. One more day walking in the sun and now not even urine to drink.

• • •

Only place to go, only place to hide now is the jungle. But inside is many thorn, so sharp it rip the clothes, cut the skin; and so many tree—palm tree, banana tree, banyan tree, bamboo tree—so thick the daytime in here is dark like night. And vine everywhere—some fat like the chest of a man, some skinny, like old lady fingers, crooked, growing crazy, grabbing our feet. Tangle so thick not even a breeze can get in.

How I will ever find my sister in here, I don't know.

We not the only ones hiding in the jungle. At night sometime we can smell, just a little, a cooking fire somewhere. No way to know if it's close or far. Cambodian or Vietnamese.

The jungle in the daytime is hot, like oven, at night, damp and cold. With no straw mat, no blanket, we dig into soil and cover ourself with old leaf, old branches. But our teeth, our bones, they chatter so loud I think maybe the Vietnamese can hear.

Sombo always sleep now with the little ratcatcher boy to keep him warm. I think Sombo also like this kid special, like sort of favorite. But also I know Sombo need to keep this kid who catch our food alive. So the rest of us can stay alive.

• • •

A million mosquito, like army, attack us all the time now; and some kid, they have the fever. Sweat like rain on them, then shiver so hard their brain is shaking inside the skull. The little ratcatcher boy now has the fever; and Sombo cover him with leaf, with stick, with his own shirt even, and go off in the jungle with his radio. And me, I follow Sombo, always watching.

His radio dying now, but Sombo lick the end of the battery and hold it to touch the other one, and for one minute his radio talk. It is the voice of Angka, saying victory is near, saying soon the Cambodian army will march into Vietnam as conqueror. Then the radio goes dead, and I see for the first time Sombo really has worry on his face.

Long time now we been hiding in the jungle, sometime we join up with other fighter, sometime we by ourself. The other fighter, they don't talk to us, but I listen to what they say to each other. Thailand. All the time I hear this word. *Thailand, Thailand, Thailand.* I don't know what's this place. But one soldier, he tell the other, if you want to get there, you go where the sun set.

Next day that guy is gone.

Sombo says we have to go north. Big fight with Vietnamese coming in the north. All soldier have to come. I don't know what's north, but Sombo, he make us walk along a stream.

One day we beg him to let us get in the water. Leeches there and also poison fish, but we don't care. So Sombo say okay. This water very cool and also very clear. I see under the water a stick, very pale. I move, it move. This stick, it's my leg. All this time I see many other skinny kid, leg like stick; first time I see my own body also is skeleton.

Now all the soldier heading north; we see other platoon in the jungle. Sometime we stop and camp, sometime we just pass each other. All the time now I look for my sister. Then, like it's miracle, we pass her group.

I run to find her and see her on the ground, lying still, her skin, her eyes, everything yellow now from sickness, almost dead. And dirt all over her—on her face, her clothes—like people walk on her. I say her name, and she open her eyes very big; but she can't talk, can't move.

Inside my head I go a little bit crazy. I touch her face and talk about how it will be when the war is over, how we can climb trees, eat ice cream, how she can get a new dress, how she can teach me to swear; but inside my head I think what really will happen. If the Vietnamese find her, they will rape her, they cut the throat, the ear. If wild animals find her, she will die slow while they eat her.

Now my hand is on my gun. Because I know I should kill her by my own. So she won't get rape, get eaten by tiger. I touch her cheek and push close her eyes with my hand. I touch the trigger and pray to our ancestor for help, to forgive me for killing this little girl, this only person left for me in the whole world.

But I don't do it. I just walk away.

I walk, stumble, my leg like no bone in them, then walk again. This is the only thing to do. Keep walking.

Big battle happen. Lotta kid get killed. Lotta soldier, too. One time I stand up and wait for the bullet to come for me. Why they don't hit me, I don't know.

Even if I want to die, I can't.

Survive. That the only thing I can do.

Sombo take us deeper into the jungle. Always it seem we walk to join the other fighter. But now we don't see the other soldier, and I think maybe he taking us a different way, maybe to get away from the war. Maybe to Thailand.

Deep in this jungle we come all of a sudden to small village next to stream. Not a real village, like before, but maybe ten hut made of stick and also mud. Like hideout, this village, with family, children, everyone living here secret.

They see us coming and the mother, she grab the baby and run to the bush and hide. The men, no gun, make begging face and say only, "Please, please," hands like praying. "Please don't hurt us."

Then one guy, he come running to Sombo and give him a gift: one bottle of Coca-Cola. Crazy, to see this soda in the jungle after all this time living like animal, nothing modern, nothing from outside world. Sombo make a frown face, like maybe he can't trust these strange hiding people, but the little ratcatcher boy, he beg Sombo to take it. So we take this soda and walk on, leave these people alone, with Sombo shaking the head like maybe a little bit angry, a little bit confuse.

That night we sleep near the stream farther away. Sombo open the soda, banging on the top with his gun; and we all stand around drinking this thing, this sweet drink that squirt out everywhere like crazy. Four years almost, nothing to eat but rice, and rat and cricket, and now in the jungle we have Coca-Cola.

That night, while all of us dream of soda bubble, a bomb land near our campsite. Sombo grab us and tell us to jump into the stream to hide. One kid, he can't swim. He stand there and cry; but the rest, we jump in the water and hold on to branch, on to each other. Piece of bomb hit the water, sizzle, so hot from explosion, sizzle all around us in the water; but no one get hit. After, we get out and see the boy who can't swim, lying dead, his mouth open like still crying.

Sombo very angry now. He doesn't say it, but I know he think the people in the hiding village tell the Vietnamese where we are. He says he gonna go back to that village, warn them that Vietnamese are near. He ask me to come; but I say no, I don't feel good, because now I'm afraid what he will do. But I follow him, always watching.

Full moon this night, and I can see Sombo, also the face of the village people he ask question. They say no, they good Cambodian, not helping the Vietnamese. But Sombo, he doesn't believe it; and I hear, very quiet, wet, slicing sound, the bayonet going through the skin. One by one he kill the people, the mother, even the baby, always very quiet, with bayonet, or maybe just hit on the head with the rifle, silent, so no one can hear.

Now no one left in the world for me. Sombo, this guy who is like big brother to me, three year protect me, save me all the time, I see he like all the other Khmer Rouge, killing easy, killing with no heart, killing even little baby. Long time I been on my own, but now really I'm alone. I survive the killing, the starving, all the hate of the Khmer Rouge; but I think maybe now I will die of this, of broken heart.

I think to run away, to live alone in the jungle, but I know Sombo can find me, that he can figure out why I run away, because I saw what he did. So I stay with the group, maybe couple day more, then run away. Also I stay a few day because of the fever. I have it now, drench with sweat in the day, cold as a stone at night. Maybe a few day I'll be stronger, ready to live on my own.

Little ratcatcher boy, he very sick now. Eyes yellow, burning all day from fever, shake all night. Sombo, he watch this kid very careful, give him little extra soup. But now this boy, he doesn't wake up. His eyes roll back inside his brain; his body droop like a dead flower when Sombo pick him up.

"You in charge now, Arn," Sombo say. He put this kid on his back, and the boy groan like his bone hurt from moving. "Five day maybe it will take me to carry him to the border, cross the river. To Thailand. I get him to hospital there, then I come back and find you."

Why Sombo gonna leave us all a sudden, I don't understand. Why this kid not just die like all the other? Maybe because he Sombo favorite. Or maybe because Sombo have a plan he not telling us about.

Beside, how Sombo can find this place, Thailand, I don't know. How he can find the way back to us, I don't think is possible.

I think maybe to go with him, or maybe to follow him, behind, very silent, till I see this Thailand. But this Sombo not like the old Sombo. This Sombo who can kill a little baby but still love the little ratcatcher boy, I don't understand; I don't trust.

So I look at him and think maybe this the last time I see him, this person who now I'm afraid, who now I think can maybe kill me, too, if I don't do what he say. And I say, "Okay, brother, see you later."

CHAPTER ELEVEN

AFTER SOMBO LEAVE, OTHER KID ARE FIGHTING OVER WHICH way to go. They finally pick one way; I go the opposite. They don't notice I sneak away. They don't care—now everyone just walking to live, not caring where we go, who live, who die.

All I think is Thailand. I walk the direction to Thailand, one day, two, maybe three, sometime even at night, always walking to where the sun set. But this jungle so dark, you can't even see the sky; you just keep walking.

One week maybe, I come to a stream. Thailand! To get to Thailand you have to cross a river; I know this from what Sombo say. So now I am almost at Thailand. All I have to do, cross this water. I walk a little more, up and down this stream, looking for shallow place to cross.

In the wood ahead I see strange thing, hut made of stick and mud. On the dirt, trail of blood. Then bodies. Old man, mother, child. I know this old man. He the one who give Sombo the Coca-Cola. These bodies, these the people Sombo kill from the hideout village. And I understand two thing: these people, they not die right away; they crawl till they die. The other thing: I been walking one whole week and only came back to the same place.

No food, no water for a long time now. Up high, where I can't reach, is fruit, green fruit I never saw before. Make me even more hungry to see this fruit I can't have, so I walk only looking at my feet. Till one time I see this fruit on the ground. Fallen down, maybe. I rush to this thing and bite it, so sweet, so juice, like heaven. Then I look at it, and it's all maggot inside. Small maggot, many, many, crawling deeper in the fruit. But too bad, I eat some already. So I eat the rest.

Today walking, I step on something sharp, something white. Human bone. Small. Scatter around. Maybe some other kid also who was looking for Thailand.

• • •

New thing to guide my way. Sound of fighting. Very far, but beat steady like a heart. I hear that noise, I go the other way.

Tiger live in this jungle. They smell the human, they smell dinner. So nighttime, I climb up in one tree—banyan tree with low branch like hammock—and hide there and maybe sleep.

I come down in the morning, grass under the tree all flat, all push down, like maybe the tiger, he sleep there, too.

So tire now, each time I step forward it take all my strength only to lift my foot. I say to myself, "Just one more step, then you can rest." Then I trick myself and say, "Okay, Arn, now one more."

Lotta monkey in the jungle. Monkey, they like to throw food at each other; I think maybe it some kind of game. So I stand under the tree where, up high, the monkey play and wait for them to maybe drop food on me. I make monkey sound, monkey face down on the ground, and they do it; they drop food on me. I don't know what it is, but I eat it.

Maybe I get sleepy from all that fruit. Maybe I sit down and rest under the tree. Because I open my eye and see little monkey on the ground, looking at me. One monkey, then two. Then many monkey. Many monkey eye looking at me. All curious. They look at me. I look at them. They talk, but I don't know what they say.

One guy, the biggest guy, he stare me in the eye. This guy, the boss, he take care of all the monkey—the mothers, the babies, and the old one. All the monkey, they live together like family. I see a mother and baby hold each other, and I think they lucky, very lucky.

One monkey, a small guy, he come over to me. Up close, he look a little bit human. Like old man. He just a baby, but he have hand and face like an old man. I hold still, and he climb on my lap. He put his arm around my neck, and he hold me like he hold his mother. I put my chin on his head and smell his fur, a smell like dust and maybe milk. His little heart beat right next to mine, fast; and he look up at me, like he know me. I keep very still so this can last forever.

Then the others start to leave, and he move a little. He watch them go, then finally, he jump off my lap. The others are all gone; this little guy, he's the last to go.

I grab him. I twist his neck and kill him. I feel very bad. I feel not like a human. Like beast or something. He give me his food and he hold me like he hold his mother, and I kill him.

Why? Why I'm so bad? He don't do anything to me.

But I need to survive. I need to eat. Before, I kill human being, and now I kill this little animal. Why?

Because every minute I have to think about surviving. Every minute.

Chill very bad now at night. Teeth chatter, bone shake, even my brain, it shiver in my head. Also blister everywhere. On my back, my shoulder, my chest. Big blister, big as my hand, so sore it hurt even to lie down. So I walk. Daytime. Nighttime. All I can do. Walk.

That monkey family, I see them in my mind all the time now. They throwing rock at me now, not food, rock and stick and shit; they throw their shit at me and scream at me. Scream about the baby. "Where the baby," they say, like human talking. "What you do to our baby?"

This screaming now, it sound like laughing, like crazy laughing, like insane. Then the monkey family, in my mind, they turn into my own family—all my sister, my little brother, my aunt—everyone laughing, playing a game, peeking from behind the tree; and I run to them, crying so happy, but they gone. Only laughing from behind the branch, laughing at me, like teasing, like they saying "Come find us." And I think maybe they dead, they calling me to come with them.

I talk to them; I say each name. And I say, "I will see

you again, I will see you again." Over and over I say this, like chant. And my family, then, all the voices join; and now all my family saying it, the whole jungle saying it—the leaf, the vine, the tree, the bug, the dirt—the whole jungle is chanting, "See you again, see you again, see you again."

Now the jungle, it slide sideway, then tip up in the air, and the tree all upside down, very crazy, very funny; and I feel, finally, happy and also sleepy and very good, warm, finally no chill, and my face is touching something warm, something soft, and I think: okay, Arn, now you can rest.

Strange thing, death. Bad taste in my mouth. And the world, it look dark, not like nighttime, like shadow and dark cloud. And dirty. Also hard to breath. Because my nose, one side, it cake with mud. And my eye, also, one is cover with mud. Like I'm bury. Then I understand. I'm living still. Half my face is sunk in mud, and I am lying on the ground. Alive.

Not even when I think I die, do I die.

Maybe death will come if I just lie here and invite it to myself. If maybe I don't move, don't breathe. Maybe it will come gentle, not from bullet or ax or starving. Maybe like sleep, like dream—soft, little bit more each minute—maybe like not even knowing it. Like maybe my number one big sister, Chantou, her spirit can be like real girl, lead the way, her hair long like before the Khmer Rouge—long, shiny black—singing love song, wearing white dress.

And now in the jungle I see something white. Tall. This thing looking at me. Eye like jewel. Like magic, this white thing, standing in the jungle. Rabbit. White rabbit. Tall as me almost, standing up on hind leg. Like human, and also spirit, this rabbit make a daze in my head, command me to follow.

Again it's a game of hiding; the rabbit, he peek out from behind the tree, then hide, then peek again somewhere else. And I follow like not even doing it myself, like I can watch myself do this thing.

Until finally I see another magic thing: river. This river, on the other side is Thailand. I know it. Because over there, no more jungle. Across the river, no tree, no vine, everything open. Sky. And grass. And dry.

And strange. And dangerous. No place for hiding, not like the jungle, which protect me all this time and hide me now from this too-bright sun, this open country, this Thailand. All this walking, I think, to get to this place, and I want only one thing. To stay where no one can see me.

But the rabbit, now he on the other side of the river. He look at me with his jewel eye, and he make a daze in my mind; and now I am strong as a hundred boy, as ox, as tank. I watch my foot go into the water, then my leg, my waist, my chest, my neck, my chin; and the body I see in the water, so pale, so thin, like only bone, like bone of dead boy in the jungle. I watch this body floating, my mind also floating, until finally I am on grass, Thailand grass, my eye aching from this too-bright sun.

And me, a soldier who kill every day, me, with body, with heart like old man, I crawl like baby.

CHAPTER TWELVE

MY BIG SISTER CHANTOU, THE OLDEST ONE, IS STANDING OVER me, chewing herb, then putting it on the blister on my back. Also my number two big sister, Maly, the one with the long black hair, she also here in Thailand and putting the medicine on me. And even my little sister, Sophea, the one I see in the jungle like skeleton, dirt all over her, eyes yellow, the one I almost kill on my own, she live also somehow. And I try to say to these three girl, "It come true! I see you again."

But the girl, they giggle; and this sound—girl laughing—is music to me, beautiful music. And they pick me up and carry me, all the time giggle, and I fall asleep to this heaven sound.

• • •

My sister gone when I wake up. Still I'm lying on this grass, Thailand grass, but shady now, in like small forest, voice all around. Voice and also feet, feet walking by. I reach for one foot, and the person scream and run away. Now another pair of feet come, and a voice that says, "We thought maybe you already dead."

Looking down at me is girl, beautiful girl, and I try to ask her where are my sister, but my lip so crack from fever, from no water, no sound can come.

"We carry you here from the border, me and my two friend," she says. "But you didn't move, for maybe five day."

This girl now I see is not my sister, is only a girl. The other girl, giggling, also come to look at me, and I understand that rabbit, he play a trick on me.

These three girl, these angel girl, they come many time and chew herb and put on me, give me a little water, and every day I get a little bit more strong. I think maybe it's a small village where I am, like the hideout village in the jungle; but not enough energy in me to ask question, even to say thank you.

Strange voice wake me up. Like machine, this voice, saying same thing over and over. This voice is bullhorn. And

152

I think maybe I'm inside a nightmare, that everything—the rabbit, the river—not real, and really I'm back in my hometown and Khmer Rouge truck is driving around telling all of us the Americans are coming, and the killing, the starving, the war, it start all over again.

I listen hard, and now I understand this bullhorn voice. It says, "All refugee, come out from hiding. Safe now to come out. Come to refugee camp. Medicine for you. Food. Water."

I know what this is, this Vietnamese soldier, like at the toy village, telling everyone to come for free food only so they can kill them. The angel girl, they giggle and run to this bullhorn voice; and now I have strength, strength for these girl who save my life, to stop them, to tell them don't run. I get up, very dizzy, my head like heavy rock, my neck like only blade of grass. But I stand and see these girl and many other people coming out of the forest and run; everyone run. And I only can close my eye now and listen and wait for the gunshot, the screaming, the moaning.

But what I hear instead is music. Cambodian love song. Song call "Waiting for You." Cambodian rock star, guy like Elvis, singing like before Khmer Rouge, like from my aunt radio, little radio tie with twine, singing to me, saying, "No matter where you are, I'm waiting for you here."

And I go to this song, like walking asleep, closer, closer all the time to this sound, until I see where it come from. Big bus. Bus with all the people running to get in. Angel girl and everyone from the village where feet go by me every day. All these people getting on the bus. And so I do it, too. I get on this bus that sings out to me, that says, "I'm waiting for you here."

It's a big bus, nice bus, with fan, maybe air-condition, and I shiver, shiver the whole time. Thin clothes, also chill from sickness, I only can grab my arm to make the shaking stop. And I look out the window with big eyes. I see Thai people wearing different clothes—not black—color clothes. Bright color. Red. Yellow. Orange. Boy in jean. Girl in short pant. Not like Cambodian girl, always button all the way up.

Window so tight, no noise from outside can come in. But inside, inside is music. Old song. Cambodia song. Love song. "Wherever you are, I wait for you," the song say. The bus driver, he have microphone and he sing it, and all kinda voice sing along. Old man like frog voice. Old lady like cat. Terrible racket, this bus, this crazy, happy bus, thumping down the road full of singing people; but to me the most beautiful sound I ever hear.

And oh, so much hunger in me, a greedy, greedy hunger to be like these people, to sing the old song, the song I kill in my heart, my heart that now is ache, that now is so swole I think my body cannot hold it, my body that now is shaking so hard I think my bone will break, where now something inside me break open and I taste salty tears on my lip and hear my voice, my own voice. Singing.

CHAPTER THIRTEEN

POWDER MILK. EVERY DAY HERE AT THE HOSPITAL—TENT, OPEN side—they give us powder milk with water. I drink it then vomit it up. Or shit it out. Like before, at the temple with the mango grove, I shit five hundred time a night; a thing like liquid is all that comes out. The food here, not real food, just water color white. Like Khmer Rouge food, this Thailand food.

Not enough cot, some kids on the ground, on little stone, crying, moaning. All of them too sick to even steal my bed when I go to the latrine. Sometime I don't even make it there. Sometime the shit just come out, and I lie in the bed and let the fly crawl all over me.

But always the nurse, she come back. With more powder milk.

I ask the nurse one day what day it is. She tell me Sunday.
I say no, what day in the year. March, she tell me. March
1979.

Four year I been away from home. Four year since I
sleep in a bed. Four year of killing and fighting and starving and dying. I think now I am maybe fifteen year old.

One night I wake up and hear a hundred thousand bullet
hitting the roof. Quick, I feel around for my gun, but only
thing near my hand is sheet, white sheet. Hospital sheet.

I listen hard for sound of battle coming, bomb falling,
people crying; my nose quiver for the smell of gunpow-
der, to see if enemy is close or far. But the only smell is
soil, soil turning to mud. It's a smell I know, of earth,
of rain, a planting-soil smell, a smell of monsoon. And I
understand. Raindrop is hitting the roof.

One hundred thousand raindrop.

Only raindrop.

Special visitor here today. Lady with pink skin, long nose.
White lady. Lady with kind face, she come and lean over
me, smelling like flower. American.

And very important person, this visitor, I think,

because all the nurse, all the doctor follow her around to each bed. Missus Carter, this, they say, Missus Carter, that. And also I learn new American word after she leave. *First Lady.* She call the First Lady, maybe because she the first lady to come see this hospital; but I think also this mean she is high ranking, like princess.

Here at hospital radio is always on. Sometime in a strange language, maybe Thai; but all the time I listen for news about Cambodia, about the war, about when it can be safe to go home, look for my family.

Sometime the radio, it's Voice of America talking. Speaking Khmer, telling all people in Cambodia to go to Thailand, war is almost over.

But in my mind I hear Khmer Rouge radio, the voice of Angka, always saying the same thing, that war is almost over.

All the same. All lies. War is here, too, where kid still are screaming from nightmare, dying every day.

More powder milk. More shit. More rain. More high-ranking visitor. This one a big American man. Pink face, nose like ax, sideburn like Elvis. Jeans, business shirt, and fancy watch. Maybe the First Man. Not sure what this guy is. Not doctor, but always hanging around the hospital, asking question, pester the nurse, pester the doctor, very worry about the sick kid, very angry if one dies. And every time he cry, like he the father of each dead kid.

I wonder if maybe he have kid back home in America. If together they ride in a shiny car, big, with radio playing rock 'n' roll. And Coca-Cola and bell-bottom pant. And maybe a pet bird like Hong have.

Pain in my gut is like snake twisting. Curling, twisting, making poison in me. Death is coming to me slow here at this hospital, just like kid in the field who die from starving, from malaria. After all I been through—fighting, bombing, running lost in the jungle—now it's death for me anyhow. So now I say good-bye to my family. I say, "Sorry I can't make it, sorry I can't come to find you; this pain is too much." And I talk to Death. Old friend after all this time, I tell Death, "You can come get me now, but please come fast."

Tonight rain is coming hard, so hard it's like flood, and the kid on the ground screaming, crying, water in the mouth, the nose, drowning, and all the doctor and nurse trying to pick the kid up, get them away from this flood; but oh, the kid crying still. You pick them up too fast, too hard, they can die.

And I see the American man walking through the hospital, his face cover in rain, or maybe tears. Now getting closer, closer to me, but he doesn't see me. So I do it; I make myself fall off the bed so he will pick me up.

But still he doesn't see and now his boot is coming at me, coming at my face; and this giant man, now he's gonna step on me and kill me, so I put my arm out, I stretch my arm up to him and now his boot goes away. He bend down now and stare at me like scared, like he thought maybe already I'm corpse and frighten of my arm coming up. Then he lean over and pick me up, very gentle, very strong. And carry me away before I pass out.

This American man, the First Man maybe, he sit at my bed now every day. A soak rag on my head and he all the time praying. "Jesus. Jesus," he says. This Jesus, I hear about him before in my town; he's like head monk in the US. So I think maybe this guy is like monk, like Jesus monk.

So sad on his face, so worry. Then all of a sudden angry. Like storm cloud. He yell at the doctor, make the doctor come over, and then he shout at him some more. Jesus one minute. Hell, damn next minute. Strange guy, this monk.

This guy, now he sneak me medicine. Not enough for other kid, he tells me, so eat it quiet. He say I have worm in me, worm that eat my food. Whatever I eat, the worm eat; but if I take this medicine, all the worm will die. Now all the day I take this medicine, my body shake like crazy; all the worm dying inside me make me shake more than ever, until finally no more shaking, no more fever, no more shitting like water.

And this monk, he speak a little Khmer. He tell me he pick me to live. Says he wish he can save all the kid; but me, I'm the chosen one. I don't know exact what this mean, but one more time I'm lucky.

New clothes. The white Jesus guy, he give me new clothes. Color pant—blue—and white shirt. He cry when I give him my old clothes—thin, gray, too big now I'm so skinny—these Khmer Rouge clothes, stiff with blood and dirt and smell of death. He burn them, but all the time, I smell death in the flame. Stench of corpse, rotting egg smell of girl with the black leg, burn meat smell of body on fire. This monk can cry, but not me.

One month, maybe two, I been in the hospital. The white Jesus monk, every day he come and feed me by his own hand until one day the doctor says I can go to the children center. I don't know what is this thing, but it look like prison camp; all the kid sleep together in big tent, no mother, no father, only dirt field in the middle for meeting and small pond, all fill with rainwater. I walk to this pond and look in, deep down, for bone or corpse. Like pond near the mango grove.

Then one kid run by, yelling, and now my body is splash, splash with waterdrop, cold, and sharp; and now lotta kid, they run, jump in this pond. They play and splash and all the voices cry out, all crazy, happy, loud. They just run and jump and splash and play, not looking for bone, for corpse. They play like very happy, like never they been soldier, never they kill people, always they been kid.

Also at the children center is a mean lady who every night yell at us, "Go to bed." The kid, they call her Missus Gotobed when she not looking, and I also pretend I hate her; but really, when she say go to bed, I almost can't stand up, so tire, so in secret maybe I like this Missus Gotobed. Just a little bit.

Another thing at this children center is game. Volleyball. The kid jump up in the air and hit this ball over a fishing net. All the other kid in camp, they watch, big audience, and so I study this game awhile and see that whoever win become an important kid at the camp, become a little bit famous. The kid who win, all the other kid want to be his friend, maybe because he get extra food or something.

For three day I watch it, then I walk into this dirt

square to try this game. I make myself like invisible, just standing at the edge. All this kid hopping like cricket, all around me, and so I also jump, and in my mind I can jump higher than these silly little kid; but my leg, they betray me, no life in my muscle, like old man leg, and so all the kid, they jump, and me, I'm like stone.

And now the ball is coming to me, fast, flying through the sky like bomb, straight at me, and oh, now my muscle know what to do—to duck, to crouch low, hug my knee to my chest, tuck my head in my arm. And wait for the blast. But only sound is little thud in the sand where this volleyball, it land at my feet.

Next sound is kid laughing. Laughing like crazy-monkey laugh, like a hundred crazy monkey, while I walk away making grim face, tough face, like the face long time ago, the three Khmer Rouge soldier I try to teach soccer in the schoolyard. I make this stone face to all these stupid kid.

All except one. One kid, every day I see hiding under a table. This kid, very small, name Runty, I see him these three day, crouch there like hiding, like waiting for bomb to fall. Now I go to this kid, this kid I think was probably also soldier, and take his hand and bring him out from his hiding place. We two—me, skinny kid with old-man body; him, tiny kid with old-man face—we sit together and watch the game.

I sit with Runty and I tell myself I will learn this game, and someday when I get strong, I will play, play it like soldier, fierce, and beat all these kid, and become a star; and then I will be a little bit famous, and my family will hear about me and come to find me.

Real food at the children center. Rice, morning glory, fish even sometime, curry, and vegetable. And the grown-ups here, they say take as much as you want. I don't believe, so sometime I eat so much my stomach pain me like crazy, because maybe, you don't know, never this much food will come again.

The Jesus monk have a name. Misster Pond. I know this because he comes to the children center one time with special candy for me, and Missus Gotobed, she yell at him. This candy, Chuckle, it call. Bright color, like jewel, jelly inside, sugar outside. He give this candy only to me and tell me hide from the other kid. But Missus Gotobed, she catch him and scold him very hard. Misster Pond, she say, not good for this kid to eat sugar, and not fair to other kid.

But Misster Pond, he yell at her, tell her mind her own business, also say a curse word. Then leave.

I eat one candy and it make water come in my mouth, very delicious, but also later it make my belly swole. I save the rest, give them out, little piece at a time, to other kid. Especially I give to two kid, both top volleyball player: Sojeat, a guy who fight very hard all the time to get the ball, to be the best; and another kid, Ravi, who can do a move call spike, where you hit the ball very hard into the sand. And I tell them, "Eat this candy, eat it slow, and remember me. I'm the kid who give you this good treat."

Almost two hundred kid in this place. All orphan. I hear Missus Gotobed say this one time to another worker. "All these kid have no parent," she say, "no relative. We check very hard, ask everyone." But I don't believe it. Out-side the children center is many, many tent. In row, like small city. Maybe ten thousand, maybe twenty thousand, maybe one million people out there in this refugee camp.

"Danger out there," say Missus Gotobed. "Stay away. Stay always on this side of the fence." But on the other side also maybe is my family. Maybe my mom. Or my aunt. Or my sister. Or Siv or Kha or Mek.

So one day when Missus Gotobed not looking, I sneak out the fence and walk up and down the row.

Family. Mother, father, kid together living. Cooking, playing game, like never they heard of Khmer Rouge. Now, like on the bus, I have this hunger, this greedy, greedy feel-ing to have what they have. Mother, sister, brother. And now my eyes go crazy, looking everywhere, this way, that way, for maybe one person who is my family. And my eye play a trick, like every girl I see is my little sister Sophea, every boy, is my brother. Until I get close and I see this is someone else family.

Then one guy I see, he smile at me like he know me, and I feel my heart now explode from my chest because this guy know me and I know him, he's guy from my old town, and he can tell me where is my family. I run to this guy, flying, and now I almost can smell the fish stew my aunt make, and I almost can hear chime of gong floating into our house in the morning, sound of gong and monk chanting to wake me up, and now I know all this sadness, all this time of being lonely, now it's over, all this time I wait and hope and walk in the jungle and keep my family lock in my heart, now finally, we will be together again, together forever, never ever again apart, and I can tell my aunt, "I do like you say, I bend like the grass, and now look, here I am."

And now this guy, he smile very wide, like he can't wait to tell me this good news, so wide, I see all his teeth. And his gum. Black gum. Like dog. Like Khmer Rouge I see one time on the horse. Like Khmer Rouge who think I'm Khmer Rouge.

This guy now, he wink at me. And my heart stop. Because this guy *is* Khmer Rouge. Guy who I bring letter to one time.

All around I look and I see Khmer Rouge, not wearing black pajama but wearing normal clothes. Smoking, playing card, napping. Like they never been soldier. Like they never kill. Never hit with the ax or shoot, or starve kid, or eat the liver of a dead man.

Khmer Rouge living in this refugee camp. This the danger Missus Gotobed talk about. This why there is a fence.

My leg want to run, twitching they want so bad to run. But very slow I turn and walk back to the children center, like just out for a stroll. Because whole place is crazy, like whole new Year Zero, where nothing ever happen before, where everyone forget everything that went before. Where even the killer can get food and tent and live right next to regular family, and everybody act like normal. Crazy place where to stay alive you also have to play this game.

Volleyball now is my life. All day, every day, I study this game. Then at night when everyone else in bed, I sneak out and practice the jumping, the hitting, the move call spike. I do all these move at night when no one can see until I get good, very good. Next time I play, no kid will laugh at me. Next time, those two top player, Sojeat and Ravi, they will want me on their team.

● ● ●

War still going on in Cambodia. We can hear it sometime in the middle of the night, pounding, far away, pounding, like heartbeat. These night Runty, he come sleep in my bed, like old time with Mek. I hold Runty like maybe father or big brother, and he stop shaking.

Today I join the volleyball game. I don't wait to be ask; I just go. And I do it: I jump, I hit, I spike, and now no one laughing. Now all I hear is clapping. Not like in Khmer Rouge time, everyone start and stop at the same time. Real clapping, cheering. A sound I like. Very much.

Misster Pond now come every day to see me play volleyball. Missus Gotobed, always she watching, and I know what she think: not fair to other kid. So I pretend like I don't see him. I play hard, to impress him, but also I pass the ball to other kid, and after the game I show these kid to Misster Pond.

One day he says to me, pick two favorite. Runty is my favorite; but he too scare all the time and not very good volleyball player, so I pick two boy: Sojeat, number one player, very competitive guy, and Ravi, tall guy who can spike but a little shy. And Misster Pond tell us three to meet him at dark at the fence for special treat.

When dark comes, we slip away from Missus Gotobed and see Misster Pond at the fence. He have a car, a big Mercedes, and he says, "Get in the trunk." Sojeat and Ravi not want to go with this guy they don't know outside the fence, where Missus Gotobed says is danger. They just kid, not ever been a soldier like me, so when someone says danger, they afraid. "Why we have to hide in the trunk," they say. "Why we can't sit in the car?" I also have a little fear, but I can't show this fear. Not to these kid, these volleyball star.

So I jump in the trunk and wave good-bye to them. I make a joke about how Misster Pond is driving me to America and no one else can know. The two boy, they look at each other; and maybe because now I'm a little bit famous at the camp for volleyball, also for having American friend, they believe me. They get in.

Not easy to breathe inside this dark trunk, bumping on the road; and the two boys, they get mad at me, say maybe this Misster Pond is bad guy, maybe he stealing us away to do bad thing to us.

Then the car stop and he open the trunk and we see that we only drive a little way, to American building close to the refugee camp. Inside all white people, pink skin, long nose, drinking beer and eating good food and playing rock 'n' roll. We eat with them, very good manner, and fall asleep with this good, full belly until it time to go home.

We sneak back and see Missus Gotobed very angry.

"Misster Pond," she say, "very bad, very dangerous thing to do with these boy. Everything I tell you, it go in your right ear and out your left."

Misster Pond, he just laugh. "They with me," he say, "they safe."

Two night later, we hear whisper and creeping outside the children center. Next day, one kid, one volleyball boy, is gone. We see him in the morning, lying in the volleyball place, his stomach cut open, fill with grass.

Missus Gotobed say this kid, he was kill by Khmer Rouge. At night they come to the camp, she say, take kid for fighting. Kid who say no get kill.

Today Misster Pond bring a special present for me and the two volleyball guy, Sojeat and Ravi. Book. American book. Child book of kid playing with dog; Judy, name of dog, I think. And also comic book call *Star War*, with kid soldier in silver uniform and animal soldier, too, very hairy, with gun. And also heavy book, no picture, call dictionary.

Sojeat always trying to compete; he grab the best one, the *Star War* book, and read the word out loud, like showing off. Ravi, he more serious guy, so he take the dictionary and very slow, he figure the word, too. Me, I take the Judy book, but the letter like worm on the page to me. So I copy the other two and say the word, too, like I figure it myself; but really all this English is nonsense to me. Sojeat and Ravi, before the Khmer Rouge time they went to school; they can read. A poor kid like me, no schooling, I dream inside the picture, myself with the Judy dog and the boy soldier in Misster Pond Mercedes in America.

Misster Pond take me and Sojeat and Ravi out again at night, and Missus Gotobed very angry. One time she follow us to the American building and yell at him. "Very dangerous, what you're doing," she says. "No going in and out at night. Thai guard can shoot you, you know? Maybe they think you Khmer Rouge sneaking in, sneaking out. Maybe shoot you, maybe even kill these kid." She says he better stop or she will have him arrest.

But Misster Pond, he just tell her to scram.

Five day after that Misster Pond doesn't come. Five day more, and now I think maybe he left for America and never I will see him again. No Mercedes, no Judy dog. I spit at the book and go play at the volleyball, very fierce, very mean, knocking kid down, hitting kid with ball, calling bad name, winning, winning, every time winning, until no one want to play with me anymore.

• • •

Missus Gotobed, she say to me, "Well, your Misster Pond make a big mistake. Maybe now he learn a lesson." She say this in a voice half mad, half happy. "Just like I warn him," she say, "he got shot by the guard."

I yell at her, call her liar, spit at her, and she just make a smirk face.

"Go see him yourself," she say, "in the hospital."

At the hospital, Misster Pond is like giant lying in kid cot. He have sweat all over his face, white bandage on his leg—and big smile on his face. Laughing, even. This crazy guy, he has couple bullet in his leg, he say, like this is big joke.

I think now I will spit on him also, this crazy man who make me care about him, give me book, tell me I'm the chosen one, and now he almost get killed. But he say Thailand queen now is very mad that guard shoot American guy. She so mad she give Misster Pond three wishes.

"I tell her what I want," he say. "Sojeat. Ravi. And you."

CHAPTER FOURTEEN

WHOLE WORLD NOW IS NEW TO ME. BIRDSONG IN THE MORNING, hoot owl at night. Hum of insect. Today even the frog, they singing to me. Because Misster Pond, he choose me to go to America.

Song in my heart now, burst to get out, so I sing it, "Let's twist again, like we did last summer," very loud on my way to breakfast, so loud even the mynah bird, he join me. I go past the swimming hole today; and this time I go to it, I stand on small log, and, not even thinking, jump, flip myself in the air. Whole world go by, tree upside down, kid face watching upside down, yelling, pointing, then—*splash!*—and only noise is bubble coming from my nose, inside this water world where it is peace and calm and where my whole life now will be happy all the time.

At breakfast, whole camp knows the news. Everyone, all the kid, they run to touch me, touch Sojeat, touch Ravi, like maybe we have magic, like maybe they can catch this magic, too.

All the kid except one. Runty. I see him hide under the table, hugging himself very tight, eyes close, head tuck in his arm. And all this happiness, all this magic, now it disappear; and my heart now turn heavy, like stone, like boulder. I push all these kid away now and run, run back to the dorm so I don't have to see Runty face, see in his eyes that I betray him.

All day I hide in bed, cover over my face, thinking about Runty, about these kid. What will happen to them? I go to America with Peter Pond, but what can they do? Live forever at this place, think only of rice, of volleyball, of more rice? And why I get to go, me who kill, who push people in the grave, do all these bad thing? All these idea put a pressure on my mind, too much thought, all fighting with each other; and all I can do now is hide, hide from these kid I love till it time to go.

Middle of the night, I feel my bed sink down a little, then something warm next to me. Runty. He come, put his arm around me like before. I pull him to me, no word to say all the sorry I feel, but he just hug me very tight. I don't even know I'm going to say this, the word just come out immediate. "I will come back for you," I tell him. "I promise." I don't know how I'm gonna do this, get him, get all these kid with no family to the United State; I just know it's true.

I fall asleep planning how I can get famous in the United State, bring these kid with me; and in a dream, all the kid they put the hand on me, push me down, down in the ground, and now I'm lying under big pile, can't move, can't get up, big weight on top of me: hundred thousand corpse.

All day Sojeat and Ravi study the English book. Me, I try to copy them, learn a lotta good new word. *Fine, thank you. How are you? Let the Force be with you!*

They write in the paper book Peter Pond give us. Me, I try the letters, but mostly I draw. Picture of my new life in America. Airplane. Peter Pond Mercedes. Eight-track cassette player. Big bowl of fish-head stew, big pile of fry ants and Chuckle candy every day.

Peter Pond is back in America now, but he send us new American clothes. Hat, glove, long pant, coat. All the kid look at this strange clothes and poke it and wonder how it work and play with it, laughing how strange America must be. But I can tell they also a little jealous.

• • •

Small flower is blooming now. Little cup, yellow, with tiny drop of water in it throat. All over the place. Cover the field, the rice paddy, the hill. Never before did I see this flower, I think. Is it only growing now, now that I'm going to the US?

I am volleyball king now in this camp. Jumping so high, like frog, I fly higher even than the net. Small guy like me, big deal to jump this high. Big deal also that I can spike. I hit the ball so hard, it fly off the dust; no one can touch it. All the kid want me on their team. Just like before I'm a little bit famous. Me and Sojeat and Ravi, we run this place; we volleyball star, we the only kid going to the US. Even Missus Gotobed, she can't tell us what to do. Always she make a sour face at me now, always she watching me with squint eye, like she think she can take away my good luck. She's the boss of this place, but she can't scare me. I already know what it feels to have real enemy. Khmer Rouge, Vietnamese soldier. Crabby old lady is nothing to me.

Today I hit the volleyball so hard it fly over the fence into the tent city. Missus Gotobed not looking, so quick I hop the fence, like cricket, pop over to get the ball before anyone can take it. Rumor going around that adult have volleyball team over there; they will steal our ball. But not if I can be fast.

All the kid looking, Sojeat, he click his tongue on his teeth. Lately, all the time he mad at me, telling me, "No tricks or we won't go the US. You get in trouble, Arn, we all get in trouble." But he's just a kid, not soldier like me, just a schoolboy, spoil and also a little conceited, so I show him I don't care what he say.

I run down this alley in the tent city, grab the ball, and start to run back. A voice call me from behind, a voice that know my name. "Little Fish," the voice say, "is that you?"

I know this voice, I know it from when my life is bullet and blood and jungle and smell of rotten flesh, and I run from it, like wind I run; I don't look to see where it come from. I run, trip on my own feet, going so fast, jump the fence, throw the ball at Sojeat, and keep running, all the way back to my tent, where I get in bed, pull up the cover, and hide.

That night, Sojeat come to our tent, make a howl sound with his mouth. "What wrong, Arn?" he say to me. "You see a ghost?"

I tell him my stomach is bad. This the truth. My stomach, my gut, now is tie in a knot. I know that voice. It know me, too. Me, the volleyball king; me, the most popular kid in this camp; me, the one Peter Pond choose to live, to go to America—that voice know who is the real me.

Kid who kill, who push people in the grave, who cook human flesh.

No volleyball for me anymore. Only study. Study English. Study number. I sit only near Ravi now, though, not Sojeat. Sojeat, he make a smirk face, ask me how is my stomach. But I don't answer. My nose in the book, now I pretend only thing in the world for me is studying.

New word I learn now: *see Judy run. Run, Judy, run.* New name I also learn: Jabba the Hut. Also, this hairy soldier cover in fur like a dog, I think is call Wookie.

Sojeat, he watch me all the time now. With careful, squinty, study eye, like when he work a math problem. Hot day, I go to the pond, he watch. Lunchtime, I get in line, he watch me. Even I go to the latrine, he watch me. This guy, he always have an eye on me now because he know my secret. He hear Sombo call to me; he know I used to be Khmer Rouge.

He can tell on me, tell Missus Gotobed about me, tell the other kid; and I don't get to go to the US.

But Sojeat a smart guy, not just book smart. He also know I'm Peter favorite. And he know if I don't go the US, maybe he doesn't go either.

He's smart. But me, I'm smarter. You can say maybe I'm a little bit like Angka, like the pineapple with a hundred eye, because me, I'm watching him, too.

I hear Sombo voice now all the time. "Little Fish, is that you?" At night I hear it in my dream. In the day I hear it every time we stand in line for meal. Food line, it goes very near the fence, so now, some day I skip the meal. Or I go very early, very late, when no line is there.

One day at lunch Missus Gotobed, she see me hide in my cot and yell at me, chase me out to the food line. She pinching my ear, pinch, pinch all the way to the fence. Where I see Sombo.

On the other side of the fence, Sombo stand, wearing normal clothes, looking straight at me.

Missus Gotobed, she still pinch my ear like she have a prize, like she now will show everyone that the famous volleyball king, really, he's killer.

Sombo, he look at me very happy, his eye crinkle with tear, but I give him a blank face. Like I can't even see him, like he not even there. He look confuse now, confuse and maybe also a little sad. One minute goes by, then two, then Sombo, he give me back a blank face. Then he turn around and walk away with another guy.

Missus Gotobed, she also walk away. But I can hear her click the tongue. Also, I can hear Sombo friend talking. "Is that the kid?" the other guy says. "The kid who can play music blindfold?"

Sombo shake his head. "No," he says, "must be someone else."

That night I lie in bed and thank Sombo in my head. One more time, I tell him, one more time, you save my life.

Peter Pond send a message. In one week we leave for America. He also send a package of Chuckle candy, twenty-dollar bill US, and important paper to carry on the trip.

The other kid now very sad, sad or mad, not look at me, not ask to play volleyball. At night, I sneak to their pillow and put the Chuckle underneath. And early in the morning, when I can't sleep, I walk by the fence, but never do I see Sombo.

Last night in camp, we say good-bye to all these kid. All crying very hard, and we crying very hard also. "You so lucky," they say. "You get to go to United State. All good thing there, free. Food and clothes and car and Coca-Cola. You so lucky." So I give each kid one American thing, some thing Peter send us: hat, shoe, jacket. Ravi, he have a soft heart, so he also give away his clothes. Then finally Sojeat, guy who always need to be better than me, he give away all his thing, too.

CHAPTER FIFTEEN

AT THIS AIRPORT, BANGKOK, IT CALL, WE SPEND OUR AMERICAN
money. Almost all of it, twenty American dollar, we
spend on ice cream.

And oh, now my stomach is pain, again like snake is
twisting inside my gut. And fever now, too, and diarrhea
and shaking. I only want to cry and scream; but if the
airplane people, they see I'm sick, they won't let me go
to the United State. So I hold it all in, stand straight like
stick; but all the thing in the airport spinning, the floor
is the ceiling, the loudspeaker voice right in my ear, and
sweat in my eye. Sojeat, he look at me angry because he
know I can ruin this big thing for him. But Ravi, he hold

me up under the arm so I can walk to the plane. And the two of us, we smile at the ticket lady, all teeth, big, big, big; and she not even notice, just take the ticket and we get on the plane.

This plane is like big movie theater, row and row of chair, maybe three hundred people inside, all push and talk Thai language, all family, mother and father and kid, and we just three kid by ourself, three kid with big badge on our chest that say PETER POND USA. And then the plane, it shake, shaking like me, like so scare. And it run very fast and all the people screaming and the plane, it tip up in the front and push me back into the seat, push my head back; and the skin on my face, on my cheek, is pull back, like in a smile. Because now we are flying.

Sojeat, he grab the best seat, the one by the window; but Ravi, now all of a sudden not so shy, he wrestle his way to also see out the window. And now we all are very excite, jumping on the seat, push and shove but in happy way, because we are going to America. Finally, the airplane lady who is the boss of this plane, she say settle down, and she tie us to the seat.

A little while later, the other boy fall asleep, but I need very quick to get to the latrine. Diarrhea and now vomit, too. Everything coming out of me, everything from Cambodia leaving me now. And so in this tiny flying latrine, stink like shit, I make a holy moment and say good-bye. To my family. To my friend. To Mek. To Runty. To all of them I say good-bye and say also, "Wait for me. I will come back for you."

The plane, now it land in a place call Denmark to get more gas, so we go outside the plane for one hour. Bright sun, all people with yellow hair, blue eye, skin like see-through. And very cold, this Denmark. Never in my life I feel cold like this. Not even in the jungle at night; this kinda cold is different, is pain.

Other people have hat, coat, scarf—all the thing Peter sent us that we give away to other kid. Shoe, too, we even give the shoe, so we freezing in this Denmark. Bare feet on the ground make us hop like cricket. And all the people, they look at us like maybe we crazy.

We go back to the plane now, running to get away from this cold; and the people—the guy who drive the plane, the lady who give the food—they give us thing— shoe, coat, itchy thing call sweater—and I have a feeling that it true what they say about the US, that white people are nice, very kind. Give you lotta stuff for free. And the lady, they pat me, the touch nice and gentle and soft, and I feel shaking because never has a girl touch me like this before. And I tell them, "Thank you," and "Let the Force be with you."

New York. The plane driver announce that soon we be in New York. I don't know any other word he say; all language like spitting and chewing talk to me, but *New York*, I know this word. A thousand people standing there waiting when we get off the plane, all family hugging, crying, waving, like holiday. We not see Peter for two month, and we not seeing him now. We wonder if maybe he forgot about us. But then he push to the front of the crowd, his face very sweaty; and in this place, so many Americans, very tall, we see Peter, not such a giant like in Thailand.

Peter car is big. Buick, he says, better than Mercedes and also with eight-track cassette player. I ask him if this his own car, and he say yes. And I think: okay, we rich now!

He is happy, too, and want to show us America. He say a lot of thing, point out the window, but only Ravi and Sojeat know this English word he saying. One word he say is *McDonald*. We going to see his friend McDonald to get something to eat. We get there, and this guy, McDonald, is wearing a hat made of paper and a nice face and so I try my English with him. "Rice," I say to McDonald. "Rice, please."

He look at Peter and laugh. "Rice," I say, very loud now. "Rice." And now Peter laugh and this guy laugh and lotta people laugh. And Peter says no rice here. No rice in

America? No one tell us this before we leave Cambodia. No rice. How we gonna live?

Then Peter says a word I hear before: *hamburger*. He get us kid each a hamburger, and we copy how he bite it. Terrible taste, like shit, and chew like old shoe. Only one thing is good: sauce on top. This sauce in little shiny envelope. I eat one, two, three, four of this sauce call ketchup, as much as I can fit in my stomach.

Driving, driving long time to get to Peter house, and many time I have to ask him to stop the car so I can vomit this ketchup. But what can I say? Only thank you; thank you for the hamburger, thank you and thank you again.

Peter mother house is big, like mansion, a hundred room, and she is old and shrivel and have a hatchet nose like Peter, and we call her grandmother; but she not smiling to us very much.

She put us in a room with a big bed, big enough to fit all three boy, and close the door. Outside we can hear her voice, Peter voice, a little bit fighting; but we think only of this big bed, very high off the ground, with cloud on top for sleeping on, white fluff fabric, soft and thick and perfect for jumping. So I jump in the air and flop myself on the bed, like doing flip in the pond. And we all do it then, jump and flop and wrestle; and we play this way a long time, because in this house it nighttime but for us it feel still like the day, the best day ever in our life.

Then Peter come in and scream at us, his face storm cloud face now, very red, little spit flying out his mouth, screaming very hard. I don't know what he's saying, but I jump in the bed, pull the cover and hide; but outside I can hear he still yelling. I think: why he all of sudden like this? Back at the camp, Peter used to love us very much and give us book and Chuckle candy, and now he's screaming and hate us.

Big mistake, I think, coming to the US.

Next morning Peter come and say, "Okay, guys, let's go." He's happy again. Last night he's so mad, now he's "Let's go, guys," and I think: this guy, why he change his mind so quickly? He take us in his Buick to a place call the mall, all kinda clothes, you put in the cart for free. Peter give us all new clothes—pant and shirt and shoe—and now I think: okay, lotta free stuff in the US; maybe not so bad here after all.

We all copy Peter: we take everything we want—hat and sock and candy and spray that smell good, like flower—and then a policeman stop the cart, and Peter yelling at us again, taking away all this good stuff we pick for our cart. "You don't do that!" he yell. "You don't do that!" Hard to understand this place, America. Hard, too, to understand who is this new Peter.

• • •

My mood going up and down now, fun time at the mall, new clothes, lure me to feel happy, then Peter yell at us and we get sour, make sour face again. Peter want to take a picture in the new clothes, and we smile, big, big, big lotta teeth; but soon as he finish, our mood sour again. And he say no picture of that bad face.

Back in the car, Peter give us a piece of paper and say learn this. He tell us, word by word, we need to learn this thing for meeting at his church. Sojeat, of course, he learn it right away. Ravi, I think he learn it too, but too shy to say out loud. Me, I just try to copy Sojeat. Long time driving, then finally Peter stop the Buick and we get out. Lotta white people on the grass, all smile at us, a little happy, a little scare also. They touch the new mall clothes we wearing. Stiff feeling inside these clothes, with tie and belt and hard shoes, like wooden, our toe all trap inside. No bell-bottom, but we proud still to have new clothes.

Then Peter make a speech, long speech, but all the time the white people, they stare at us. Sometime with sad face, sometime mouth just hang open, sometime whisper behind the hand; but always they look at us like never before they saw kid like us. Now Peter give us the microphone.

"Speak in the microphone," Peter say. "Speak it, one

or two word." Sojeat, for first time in his life, he gets shy, says he don't want to be first. Ravi, he terrify, too, and I see Peter looking like a little bit mad. So I take it; I hold the microphone like I see Elvis do, like the Beatle, and I say something from the paper Peter give us. I say I am happy to be here in the United State.

And all the people clap. They applause us for a very long time, and I have this feeling deep in me that I like this. I like this sound. Very much.

Only I been in the United State two day, and already I'm a little bit famous.

CHAPTER SIXTEEN

SURPRISE TO US, OTHER KID ALREADY LIVING AT PETER HOUSE. White kid. Peter own kid. One name Kate, one name Doug, one name Donna, all same blue eye as Peter. And a woman—Peter also have a wife, name of Shirley, a little bit old, like she can be Peter big sister, maybe. These kid, they shake our hand, say, "Welcome to America," but I can see in their eye a little bit worry, same look as on Hong mother face when he ask if I can come with them on the train, like afraid that maybe not enough food for everyone.

But inside is lotta food. Banana, orange, other fruit in bowl, just sitting out to take, not even hiding. We have a formal eating—good rice dinner, fancy plate, candle, and praying. After, me and Ravi and Sojeat, we sneak some of this fruit in our room, put it under our pillow, and save for later, maybe. But we can't wait; we eat some right away, our belly stuff and round, and also we play with the peel: we throw it back and forth like game. Before we go to sleep, we open the window and pee outside, fun thing to do, to see how far the pee can shoot. Also we afraid maybe this American latrine, this power toilet, will suck us down.

One, two, three day we live here, eat formal, rice every meal, work the ABC with Shirley. We teach Doug, Kate, and Donna how to play volleyball, how to spike, and they teach us good new swear word in English. And at night we lay our cheek on this soft pillow and listen for sound of nothing here in the dark, here in this New Hampshire, no sound at all, only the sound of this house groan a little, holding all these people inside.

One morning Shirley come in our room and yell at us very hard. She goes bazooka, all this banana peel in the room, smell bad like latrine; and I think: okay, now we get sent back to Cambodia. In the living room, she fight with Peter, crying voice and also shouting, word I can't understand; but Ravi tell me what she say. "Not my idea to bring these kid," she say.

We packing our stuff—all our clothes from the mall, ABC book—when Peter come in and say we have to have a meeting. And all of us, me and Ravi and Sojeat and Peter kid and Shirley, we all have to sit together for long meeting where we talk about what we did bad and make new rule. Also me and Ravi and Sojeat , we get new chore, like chop the wood; and I think: uh-oh, I hope this New Hampshire not gonna be like Khmer Rouge time, hard work all the time, new rule every day, long meeting every night.

In the daytime is this new life in America. Chore. Okay, I don't mind. Because also lotta good food, big soft chair call "couch," TV show, *Duke of Hazzard*, about American kid with fast car. At night, though, when all the house is asleep, Cambodia kid come to my mind, starving kid, kid like corpse, kid I left behind, orphan like Runty. Kid who die in battle, blood, brain, intestine all over. Also I see the face of people I kill myself, woman who grab my ankle and call me Khmer Rouge. And I sweat like fever and squirm so this heavy American blanket tangle and trap me like vine in the jungle until finally I get up and go sit by the window, waiting for the sun to come up and daytime to begin again.

• • •

Daytime getting shorter every day now, cold at night, almost like Denmark. We get up very early in the morning now every day, 4 a.m., do chore, chop wood, work the ABC with Shirley. Then one day Peter say it time for us to go to school. Never I been to a real school before. Ravi and Sojeat, they been before, so they only a little scare; but me, I'm terrify. This school is call "high school." All teenage kid, maybe five hundred. All white. We the only speck of brown in this big bowl of white rice. The teacher hold up a thing call globe, and point and say, "Cam-BO-de-ah. That where these kid from. Cam-BO-de-ah."

The kid, they stare at us, mouth open, then I hear a sound like bees buzzing. All this kid talking at once, all like giant cloud of bee. We wear our mall clothes—khaki pant, tie, and shirt—very proud; but these kid also wearing bad clothes, like jean, torn and patch, and the girl in tight shirt, and I wonder if maybe these kid poor, maybe we the only rich one. Also, in the hall I see them kissing. This private thing they do in public, and I look away, scare, like maybe these kid are bad, like prostitute.

This high school building also confuse me very much. Lotta door everywhere, long hall, short hall, everything look the same. So I go by accident to the girl latrine. They scream and point at me like maybe I'm criminal. So I run out, very sweaty, and I see Sojeat watching and also laughing with these American kid. Why he didn't help me? I have this angry feeling about Sojeat. And all day I hold it in. All day I also have to pee very bad, but I hold it till we get home.

Next day the teacher, she assign one of the cool kid, football player, he call, to take care of me. Big kid, shoulder like mountain, to show me where to go. I feel relax finally with this big guy for protection, and I take his hand so he can show me the way. But quick he shake me off like my hand have shit on it. So I follow him, walk behind, bee voice buzzing everywhere; but no way I can keep up with his long leg. I look for Doug, maybe Kate, or Ravi, to show me the way but see only this guy's mountain shoulder going down the hall away from me.

One word I hear all the time: *monkey*. Sound of bees buzzing mostly, but always I hear this word *monkey*. I ask Doug one night what it mean, and he show me; he jump and scratch under his arm, go *eek-eek*, but I understand already. These kid at high school, they think I'm like animal.

Inside my heart, a bad feeling grow. Like tiger growling, like a big anger, like I have when I was soldier, and I think: if they don't stop, I will hurt these American kid. I will show them what animal is.

• • •

Peter all the time obsess with Cambodia. Go to meeting all the time about it, tell us boy we now gonna speak about Cambodia to the United State. He give us a speech, make us learn it word by word, and one day say, "Okay, guys, no school today; we going on adventure." We drive a long time in the Buick, Ravi and Sojeat in the back, reading school book, English book, me up front singing rock 'n' roll on Peter radio. This is how I learn English. The other two, they read the book, get good grade in school; me, I sing along with American kid. "Copacabana," "Betty Davis Eyes," Bruce Springsteen—they my favorite.

At this meeting we wear our stiff mall clothes and speak Peter speech, not really knowing what the word mean; and after, one little girl, she come up to me and give me a dollar. "For your country," she says. This little girl, blond hair, curl, like painting in church Peter take us to, picture of angel; and I take her dollar and very careful I fold it in my pocket. To send to Runty.

And we all smile, all teeth, big, big, big and get our picture in the paper.

Couple days later, we in the newspaper again. This time bad news. Somebody setting fire in this New Hampshire, burning three barn, and the newspaper mention us, new kid from Cambodia, wonder if maybe we did it.

That day at lunch, big football player kid and other

kid, also very big shoulder, they make a circle around me, light match in my face, ask me if I like fire. All of them light match, flick lighter, and point at me; and I know they think I made this bad fire, and so I use the curse word Kate teach me. "You a fucker!" I tell them. And they laugh and laugh, a sound very high, very crazy; and I think now they the one that sound like monkey.

Inside my head I talk to them. You don't know what I can do. Before, I shoot guys like you. All my muscle, I need to hold back so I don't do what this tiger in my heart is telling me to do: kill these kid.

At night I fall asleep, dreaming I can't find the bathroom. Running through the jungle, through the high school, looking everywhere for the bathroom, and now kid from high school in my Cambodia dream. Big football player, kid who light the match, he come into my dream. I make him kneel on the ground, hand tie behind; and I have ax in my hand, and now this ax is hitting over and over, hitting this kid till now his head like only hamburger on the ground.

I try now to go back to sleep, think about all the good thing here in this good place, this rescue place call New Hampshire, United State, and think: after all the thing I been through, now being rescue is something I also have to survive.

• • •

Special class for me now. ESL, it call. Special teacher. Pat her name. Every day the other kid go to class, even Sojeat and Ravi, they go to regular school. Sojeat tease me; he call me stupid. This ESL, it in a small room, like closet almost, room with only Pat and me. All day she try to teach me this English. Try to make my mouth work this strange way. Tire, my tongue is tire; my tongue like asleep at the end of one hour. But all the time she push hard, make me learn more word.

Lotta word have this one sound I can't make: *th*. *Thanks, think, thunder.* Also this sound in the middle of some word, some very important word, like *bathroom*. Very important sound, this *th*. But we don't have this sound in Khmer. So my tongue can't do it. But Pat, she say it over and over and over. Get close to my face, closer and closer she get; her tongue, she show it to me, pushing on her front teeth, like she gonna eat me. And I spit her. Right in the face, I spit.

She jerk away from me, and I think: okay, now she gonna hit me; but she only leave the room, tear in her eye. And I think: why I spit at this person, only one trying to help me? Why I'm so bad? Why?

Something call snow here. It fall from the sky like sugar, like tiny flake of sugar, this beautiful thing out the window; it make me very sad, so sad, I just walk out the school and walk all the way home. So quiet now in this snow, like pillow on the world, and every step I think of Mek, how he say paradise is the place where sugar fall from the sky and no kid is hungry; and this snow, it land on my eyelash, wet, like tear.

One teacher here in short pant; he teach the kid to play game. Crazy. In America they have teacher for every-thing, even to teach kid to play. In Cambodia, kid know how to play, no grown-up to teach them. This game here, it's soccer. I know this game; I know this from home. I even play it one time with Khmer Rouge. So I get the ball and I run and run—so little, I can go in out the big hairy leg of American kid—till I kick it hard, and it fly in the net. Like in volleyball, like spike, like anything I ever try to do, I do it to get attention, to get a little famous. Also I do it to show I can behave good and have something I can give. I can do it, kick the ball more hard than other kid, run faster than other kid, because maybe I want it more bad. And now I'm a little bit famous. This morning, I'm monkey; this afternoon, hero.

Now the soccer teacher, he say I can be on the team; and on the bus on the way home from school, now the other kid are nice to me. Sojeat, he lean over and whisper to me. "They think you hero. But I know what you really are."

At lunch one day, big cafeteria, lotta noise, a ponytail teacher, music guy, he call my name, and I think: uh-oh, trouble now from this guy, too. "Arn," he says, "I have a present for you." And he hand me it. Small wooden flute. Song flute, like back in Cambodia.

I don't know how to play this thing, but I take it; and one night when the studying is too hard, I go out in the wood behind the house, and I try a little bit to get to know this flute. Another night I go down into the laundry and try. But, like magic, it know me. From my finger, from my mouth, the flute charm out the song, the old song from Cambodia, song I know in my soul. Love song, ancient like the famous temple of Angkor Watt, they live inside me; and when I close my eyes, they come, a little bit of Cambodia, like smell of jasmine and lemongrass, ginger and cardamom, floating in the air, in this place, this New Hampshire.

Getting a lot of attention now; Peter lotta time take me out of school to go to speak to church group, to government office, to see VIPs. Ravi and Sojeat say they don't like this speeching. Sojeat, he say he only want to be in school every day so he can get good grade and be a doctor.

And Ravi, he like America kid, not want to talk about bad thing, only fun thing. So Peter don't make them speech.

But I see they feel a little bit envy, because now all the time I get attention. I want to talk; they don't. And Peter own kid—Doug, Kate, Donna—they don't care about Cambodia, but I can see they have envy, too.

But for me, performing is something I know like old shoe, like my family used to do; now I'm onstage also, and now people applause me and give us money for Cambodia. And I think: maybe this can be how I pure my heart from all the bad thing I do; maybe this is why I survive, to get money for Cambodia. And finally, this hunger I feel all the time when I see other people family, this hunger, finally I think it can get fed.

One night, nice candle dinner. Dish and cloth and candle and pray. Peter out of town, meeting someplace; now all the time Peter goes to meeting, meeting, all for Cambodia, he says. And Shirley has a little sad in her eyes, a little lonely maybe for Peter, a little envy maybe he spend all his time on Cambodia. So I brag a little; I tell her how I score a goal again at soccer team so maybe she can be proud and not so sad, like how she smile when Sojeat, he shows her A+ on his paper.

And Shirley, she smile and say good, very good, but a little distract, and look to the front door like maybe

199

Peter will come in. And then Sojeat, he lean over to me and whisper in my ear. "You Khmer Rouge," he say. "You Khmer Rouge; you kill my mother, my father."

And then inside me, like before, in battle, something goes electric. I jump to the table like flying, standing, my feet on this cloth, this dish, standing like giant, and all the plate crashing, the glass breaking, and the little sister, Kate, she screaming and crying. I hear this, but my mind now is a tunnel, all black. I see only Sojeat face, all the proud and conceit go out of it now; and he scare, like baby, like people at the mango grove waiting for the ax to crack, like first guy I ever shoot, so surprise still grinning, like old lady in the toy village right before I kill her.

Then blood is everywhere, all over Sojeat face, his shirt, the white cloth on the table. I do it; I do something to make it come. I see blood on my sneaker, like maybe I kick him in the face; but I don't know. And people crying, Kate saying, "Oh no, oh no." But ah, blood, I remember blood: how it smell, how it spread, how it make you like drunk, like wanting more and more and more; and the tiger in my heart, it roar now, one taste of blood and it want more. So I grab Sojeat on the neck and he grab me and rip my shirt and we fall, all the dish crashing, breaking, and Kate crying, and I run into the kitchen to find a long knife, and I see my arm raise in the air—so strong, so beautiful—this arm, this knife now will speak all the thing I can't say.

And then the air, it all fly out of my body; something grab me so hard, something strong like jungle vine, it wrap around me and pull me down, down, down, more dish crashing, down to the carpet. On the ground next to me is Ravi, breathing hard and also crying, his arm around my waist. I look up and see all the family face looking down at me now from far away—Kate and Shirley, tear on the cheek, very scare, and Donna and Doug crying also. And I jump up and run out the door into the dark.

CHAPTER SEVENTEEN

ONE SHOE GET CAUGHT IN THE DOOR WHEN I RUN, SO I KICK OFF
the other and run. Wearing only my pant, my shirt, rip
at the shoulder, and no shoe, only sock, make me very
cold in this New Hampshire nighttime. Cold and cover
in blood, my white shirt soak with blood. Sojeat blood,
my blood. Sticky and smell like iron, blood on your skin
is something that soak in and never get out.

Peter family house on a mountain, no other house
around, so where I run is all tree, very many, very close,
like trapping you on every side. And now it rain, the raindrop hit the leaf like bullet, and the ground smell like rot.
And now, to me, I'm in the jungle again.

So I do what I know how: I walk. I walk and walk and walk and walk, branch grabbing at me, slashing my face, until finally, the jungle clear and now I'm on a road. Very dark now, black, like deep pond, no bottom, so only way to follow this road is to feel with my sock. Like trance to walk now on this straight, flat road, only sound is my heart pounding like gun in my chest. Only thought in my mind now is how bad I am, how never can I tame the tiger in my heart, how only thing I can do is get far away from all these people I know—people I hate, like mean kid at school; people I love, like Peter; people who try to help me, like the speech teacher—because me, I am poison; I hurt everything I touch.

All a sudden I hear loud sound coming close on me from behind, and bright light, too, flash like bomb blast. I plunge myself sideway into the grass, and then a big wind roar by, so strong I think it will suck me inside. Then I understand. This wind, it's a truck going by.

But still only thing for me to do is walk. Walk on the highway and think what to do. No way I can ever go back to Peter house again after this bad thing I did. And no way to get back to Cambodia. No matter how hard I think, is no way out. Until, finally, I feel my mind hoping.

Hoping for another truck to come. And hoping now to feel nothing anymore, no pain, no anger, no shame. No more kid teasing me at school, hive of bee calling me monkey; no more frustrate from a tongue that can't say English, a tongue that can't say what really in my heart. No more nightmare of corpse, of blood, of killing. Hoping only for truck, for feeling of tire, big fat truck tire, rolling over me, making me go away, disappear, no more Arn, only a black stain on this black road.

Then I see ahead is small village, all dark, all window black, everyone sleeping, traffic light even it just blink the eye very slow; and I feel sleepy, sleepy and wish only for my soft pillow, my soft bed at Peter house. I keep walking into this town, thinking of all these New Hampshire people—so warm inside their house, wrap in blanket, dreaming in their bed, dreaming their American dream of mall and McDonald—and me outside, teeth chattering, no idea what to do.

Flashing sign ahead says TV. This a word I know for sure. Sign also says FREE. This word I learn after the mall, so I know what's for pay, what's for free. Also a word I don't know: MOTEL. But I understand Free TV at this place, and my feet just go there. The door like magic, it open, slide apart, whoosh me inside. No TV, no people, only a counter and cash register like at the mall, but warm, warm like Cambodia, where air is like your own skin, so warm that I just lie down on the carpet and go to sleep.

• • •

I don't know what time it is, but I feel people step around me, business shoe go past my head, shiny, black, very hurry these shoes; and I wake up, startle, a man yelling, "Get out! Get out!" I jump up, see now with clear eye my white shirt cover in blood, and run out the magic door into the cold again. Cold and still a little dark, gray, like the whole world is shadow. And foggy, also, like big cloud floating on the ground so you can't see in front of you.

Into this cloud I step, my hand out in front so I can feel where to go, but I see only more fog, fog and shape of people. I see my sister, my little brother; I see people walking to the mango grove—the old music teacher, the prisoner with hands tied behind—people that been shot, people I kill, all ghost, floating, just floating by me.

Sound of walkie-talkie now, crackle with voice talking, and I see in this fog a police car. Police now come to shoot me, to kill me for all these bad thing I done, and I think: when the bullet hit, will I look like all the other people, where the begging stop, the hope die in their eye, and the calm come, the waiting? I wonder what the bullet will feel like when it hit: like relief? like joy? like nothing?

But the police, he doesn't see me; he look right at me, not seeing me, and drive by. I laugh a little at him, laugh out loud. Stupid police. How he can find me if he stay inside the car? To hunt someone you have to get close, smell their sweat, not hide inside your big American car.

So now it my job to hunt him, to find him in this fog, to go to his gun, to call it to me, to bring the bullet into myself.

I step out from this cloud, and not too far away I see a red light flashing; police car is stop up ahead, and the police, he's shining a flashlight around. I walk to this light, fast, no stopping, no time for thinking. The police, this time he see me; he point his light right in my eye.

"Don't move," he says.

I keep walking.

"Don't move," he put his hand on his gun. "Stop."

I don't stop; I walk to him, straight to him, closer, closer, until finally I can smell him, smell the coffee, the leather of his belt, the hair oil. I put my arm around him, lean my head on his chest. "Take me home," I say. "Please."

Peter, he wrap me in a blanket, crying. Shirley also crying, everyone crying except Sojeat; his face very swole, his eye still full of anger for me.

Peter take me to his room, close the door, and I get ready now for the beating. But Peter, he just hug me very tight, hold me very close long time, rock me side to side like a baby.

"Thank God, thank God," he says.

How I can tell this guy, this guy who give me all this good thing, this guy who save my life, how I can tell him

I think all the time about people who die, people I kill? He take me outta the camp, and I think I can leave all this death, leave all these people, leave them in Cambodia. How I can tell him they follow me here? How I can tell him, "You a nice man, Peter, but, me, I'm bad"? All I think is: I want to die. I want to kill.

"It hurt," I say. The words in Khmer, they just come out.

Peter make a worry face. "What hurts?"

I point at my chest. "My heart. Like a tiger," I tell him. My heart, like a tiger inside, clawing my rib to get out. So much hate in there it hurt. Hate for the people who kill my family, hate for the people who kill my friend, hate for myself.

"Why I live?" I ask Peter. "Why I live and so many people die?"

"I told you," Peter says. "You're the chosen one."

I don't understand.

"Arn, you're the one who will tell everyone what happen in Cambodia," he says.

"Why?" I ask him. "My family still dead, my friend still dead, my other friend still living in the camp."

"You tell the story," Peter says. "It's a way to save people still in Cambodia, bring them to the US. But also to save yourself. Speaking out, telling the story, it's a way to choose living. To say you are with the living now. Not the dead."

This idea, it wrap around me like a warm blanket, it settle my shaking bone, it calm my heart, and I understand. All the time you fighting, you think only of how to survive. All the time you survive, you wonder why you don't die. But now my life can be something different. Now, in America, I don't have to fight. I don't have to survive. I can chose a new thing: to live.

CHAPTER EIGHTEEN

NEW YORK CITY
1984

I SWALLOW A BIG BREATH AND START. "MY NAME IS ARN," I SAY. "I'm from Cambodia."

Big speech I'm giving. My own speech, not the one from Peter. Long time I work on learning English— ABC every morning with Shirley, every day with Pat, the special teacher at school—but mostly I learn it on TV, *Duke of Hazzard, A Team*. I learn it so much I even graduate New Hampshire high school. And now I get invite to speak at big church in New York City, St. John the Divine it call. Flowing with people. Ten thousand people, Peter say, with lotta VIP, like guy name Desmond Tutu and singer name of James Taylor and guy from *New York Time*. All waiting now for me to speak.

I start very slow, very careful. I tell a little about my life before the Khmer Rouge, about doing the twist with my brother, about frogging with Hong. Then I tell about how all the people have to leave the city, about the body at the side of the road, about being force to leave my family, probably all now dead. And then the story pour out of me, about the kid dying from no food, the ax hitting the skull, the people calling to me from the grave. And then something happen. The paper I hold, big splash of water on it, the word now dripping off the page. And my voice now, my careful American voice, it crack and break and die in my throat. Never have I cry, not one time, all these year. From eleven-year-old kid till now, not one tear. So many year, I think I kill off all the tear inside me. But after this long, dry season, now finally the rain.

Nice man who introduce me, he come to my side, ask me if I want to stop. I say no, I want to finish my speech. And now all the word come; they come not careful, they come with sob, my body shaking like a fever, with tear dripping off my nose, off my chin—my shirt, my collar now all soak through—until finally I finish.

A very great quiet now, hush in this audience, silence like after we play the first time for Khmer Rouge, waiting to see if we live, we die.

Then one applause. One more, then many, many hand

all together clapping, so much applause like thunder, like the church, it roar from its bones, and oh, the sound, it lift me up, up high, like on top of a mountain, and I look out now and see all these people, American people—men and woman, boy and girl, even the guy from the *New York Time*—all these people crying, too.

And finally, the tiger in my heart, he lay down a moment and rest.

EPILOGUE

ARN CHORN-POND HAS BEEN SPEAKING OUT ABOUT THE genocide in Cambodia ever since that day in 1984. As a representative of Amnesty International and a founder of Children of War he has traveled the world, shared the stage with rock stars such as Sting, Peter Gabriel, and Bruce Springsteen. He's met kings and presidents—including Jimmy Carter, whose wife, Rosalynn, visited his bedside in Thailand.

During the 1980s and '90s, Arn returned to Cambodia many times—once to win the release of ten thousand hostages being held by Khmer Rouge holdouts. And he visited Cambodian refugees still living in camps in Thailand along with the princess of Cambodia, the woman he'd loved as a little boy, to teach the children traditional songs of their homeland.

In one of his visits home, where he organized hundreds of kids for a cleanup of the war debris in Phnom Penh, a woman approached him. It was his second oldest sister, Maly. Then, at a speech in Lowell, Massachusetts, where Arn was working with youth gangs, another woman came to the podium. It was his sister Jorami, who told him that their aunt had also survived. His aunt died soon after she and Arn were reunited. The rest of his family had perished.

Kha and Siv also survived; the other members of the musical troupe all disappeared or died. Runty was adopted by a family in Cambodia.

Sojeat and Ravi both live in the United States; Peter Pond's family eventually adopted seventeen Cambodian children.

Sombo lives with his wife and children in the northern part of Cambodia, in an enclave where thousands of Khmer Rouge remain to this day. Koong, the boy Sombo carried to the Thai border, also survived and was adopted by a family in Canada.

Arn eventually reunited with all of them. But despite searching for nearly twelve years, he had been unable to find Mek. Then one day, on a visit to Battambang, Arn saw a destitute man in a lean-to by the road. It was Mek—who had been searching just as hard for Arn. He had arrived at the Thai refugee camp just days after Arn left for the United States.

Determined to help Mek return to his profession as a musician, Arn began to search for the few other master musicians who had survived the Khmer Rouge. Using funds he raised by speaking about his experiences, Arn founded Cambodian Living Arts in 1998. Today, CLA master musicians travel throughout Cambodia, teaching children the traditional music that would have otherwise been lost.

To learn more about Cambodian Living Arts, visit www.cambodianlivingarts.org.

AUTHOR'S NOTE

OVER THE COURSE OF TWO YEARS, I SPENT COUNTLESS HOURS
with Arn Chorn-Pond—at my home during long, emo-
tionally draining interviews; in New England, talking to
his adoptive family; and in Cambodia, where we retraced
virtually every step of his life during the three years,
eight months, and twenty days of the reign of the Khmer
Rouge.

With the help of a translator I interviewed Kha, Siv,
Mek, and a number of Arn's fellow survivors as well as
"Missus Gotobed." We even traveled to a remote part of
the country still controlled by the Khmer Rouge, where
we spent a day with Sombo. I asked Arn difficult, probing

questions about his actions—the heroic and the horrific. I verified, as much as possible, the truth of his story.

Then I wrote his story as a novel. Like all trauma survivors, Arn can recall certain experiences in chilling detail; others he can tell only in vague generalities. For instance, he can describe the eerie *click* of a land mine being sprung and the hideous stink of a gangrenous leg. But he can't remember the name of the little girl who lost her leg or when or where the attack took place. So I added to his recollections with my own research—and my own imagination—to fill in the missing pieces. The truth, I believe, is right there between the lines.

Sometimes, when Arn talks about his childhood, it's as if he becomes that little boy all over again. He speaks with an urgency, a pure terror at times, that is palpable. But when he talks about the way music saved his life, about his work to preserve the traditional music of Cambodia, about his belief in the power of forgiveness—he is absolutely radiant.

Trying to capture that voice was like trying to bottle a lightning bug. Every time I imposed the rules of grammar or syntax on it, the light went out. And so, in telling Arn's story I chose to use his own distinct and beautiful voice. The end result, I hope, captures the courageous and unforgettable person he is.

ACKNOWLEDGMENTS

I FIRST WANT TO HONOR THE CAMBODIAN FAMILY I HARDLY knew: my grandfather Chhit Leung; my grandmother Yeay Heur; my father, Chhit Jawn; my mother, Ki Savinh; and my aunt, who raised me, Kiet Yeum. I honor my living sisters, Chhit An and her family, Ny Loeung, Vichhai, Bo, Vichara, Chussets, Jong, and Lap; and Chhit Anne and her family, Phat, Pha, Ramon, and Ravi; and all my other family members both dead and alive.

With much gratitude, I want to acknowledge my adoptive American and Khmer family: my father, the late Peter L. Pond, and his children; my mom, Shirley Pond, and her children; together with all my other adopted

Pond family Cambodian brothers and sisters.

And thank you to so many close friends and mentors who have, for all these years, supported and loved me, including the late Somdech Maha Ghosananda, a great friend of my adoptive father; Princess Buppha Devi of Cambodia, whom I met in the Thai refugee camps before I came to the USA in 1980, and who later welcomed me back to Cambodia when she had become Minister of Culture and Fine Arts; Judith Thompson and the Rev. Paul Mayer, who helped me found Children of War; all who helped me and my adoptive father start Cambodian Volunteers for Community Development, Judge Mark Wolf, Judy Jameson, and the late Father Cunningham, past president of Providence College; John Burt and Alan Morgan, my cofounders of Cambodian Living Arts (CLA); Charley Todd and Ingrid Martanova, past CLA copresidents; Dickon Verey, current CLA president; and all the many international CLA donors and advocates, particularly the original supporters, Martin Dunn, Scot Stafford, Wendy vandenHeuvel, Libet Johnson, Alison Van Dyk, Henry Chalfant, Alec and Anne White, Peter Gabriel and Dickie Chapel, Theary Seng, Phloeun Prim, the Burt family, and my teacher, Master Yuen Mek. Thank you to Jodi Solomon Speakers, which has represented me as a speaker for more than a decade; World Education, which embraced and gave structure to my original idea of saving the Cambodian master artists; and the Marion Institute, which manages Cambodian Living Arts today as one of their largest programs. I want to acknowledge the outstanding Cambodian musicians Chinary Ung, Sam Ang Sam, Him Sophy, and Khuon Sithisak; the artist ChathpierSath; the director of the documentary film *The Flute Player*, Jocelyn Glatzer; and the founder/director of the Documentation Center of Cambodia, Youk Chang. My very special gratitude goes to Thon Seyma, Nanda Shewmangal, and Ker Lee.

Finally, I want to thank Patty McCormick, who has brought to life the characters in this book, many of whom were children who lost their lives at the hands of the Khmer Rouge. I want to honor them with this book, and I want them to know they live on in my heart, and now, in these pages.

Arn Chorn-Pond
Cambodia, 2012